Matt had been so *different* to anyone Frankie had ever known. He'd spoken to her of ancient myths and he'd weaved magic into her being. He'd been totally unique.

"It's no joke. That weekend with you was my way of trying to ignore the reality of how my life was about to change. But I do not believe in hiding, Frankie. And so I left you in order to return to my country, my people and my role as ruler."

His words came to her from a very far way away.

He was a king.

Which meant... Oh, God. She reached behind her for the sofa, sitting down into it with a thud and drinking her wine as though it were a lifeline.

"Yes," he agreed, moving closer to her. "Our son is my heir. He is a prince, Frankie."

Secret Heirs of Billionaires

There are some things money can't buy...

Living life at lightning pace, these magnates are no strangers to stakes at their highest. It seems they've got it all... That is, until they find out that there's an unplanned item to add to their list of accomplishments!

Achieved:

1. Successful business empire.

2. Beautiful women in their bed.

3. *An heir to bear their name?*

Though every billionaire needs to leave his legacy in safe hands, discovering a secret heir shakes up the carefully orchestrated plan in more ways than one!

Uncover their secrets in:

The Secret Kept from the Italian by Kate Hewitt

Demanding His Secret Son by Louise Fuller

The Sheikh's Secret Baby by Sharon Kendrick

The Sicilian's Secret Son by Angela Bissell

Claimed for the Sheikh's Shock Son by Carol Marinelli

Look out for more stories in the
Secret Heirs of Billionaires series coming soon!

Clare Connelly

SHOCK HEIR FOR
THE KING

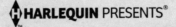

Recycling programs
for this product may
not exist in your area.

ISBN-13: 978-1-335-47834-4

Shock Heir for the King

First North American publication 2019

Copyright © 2019 by Clare Connelly

Printed in U.S.A.

Clare Connelly was raised in small-town Australia among a family of avid readers. She spent much of her childhood up a tree, Harlequin romance book in hand. Clare is married to her own real-life hero and they live in a bungalow near the sea with their two children. She is frequently found staring into space—a surefire sign she is in the world of her characters. She has a penchant for French food and ice-cold champagne, and Harlequin novels continue to be her favorite-ever books. Writing for Harlequin Presents is a long-held dream. Clare can be contacted via clareconnelly.com or on her Facebook page.

Books by Clare Connelly

Harlequin Presents

Innocent in the Billionaire's Bed
Bought for the Billionaire's Revenge
Her Wedding Night Surrender
Bound by the Billionaire's Vows
Spaniard's Baby of Revenge

Christmas Seductions

Bound by Their Christmas Baby
The Season to Sin

Harlequin DARE

Off Limits
Forbidden
Burn Me Once

Visit the Author Profile page
at Harlequin.com for more titles.

For romance readers everywhere, and especially my advance readers, who are some of the best champions and friends a writer could hope for.

PROLOGUE

THERE WERE THREE things Matthias Vasilliás loved in life. The glow of the sky as the sun dipped into the horizon, bathing the world in streaks of gold and peach; the country he was one week away from ruling; and women—but never the same woman for long, and never with any expectation of more than this: sex.

The wind blew in across the hotel room, draping the gauzy fabric of the curtain towards him, and for a moment he looked at it, his mind caught by the beauty, the brevity, of such a fragile material—the brevity of this moment.

In the morning he'd be gone, she'd be a memory—a ghost of this life. In the morning he would fly back to Tolmirós and step into his future.

He hadn't come to New York for this. He hadn't intended to meet her. He hadn't intended to seduce a virgin—that wasn't his usual *modus operandi*. Not when he couldn't offer any degree of permanence in exchange for such a gift.

No, Matthias preferred experienced women.

Lovers who were *au fait* with the ways of the world,

who understood that a man like Matthias had no heart to offer, no future he could provide.

One day he would marry, but his bride would be a political choice, a queen to equal him as King, a ruler to sit beside him and oversee his kingdom.

Until then, though, there was this: there was Frankie, and this night.

She ran her fingertips over his back, her nails digging into him, and he lost himself to her completely, plunging inside her, taking the sweetness she offered as she cried out into the balmy New York evening.

'Matt.' She used the shortened version of his name—it had been such a novelty to meet a woman who didn't know who he was, didn't know he was the heir to the throne of a powerful European country, that he was richer than Croesus and about to be King. Matt was simple, Matt was easy, and soon this would be over.

For ruling Tolmirós meant he would have to abandon his love of women, his love of sex and all that he was, outside the requirements of being King. His life would change completely in seven days' time.

Seven days and he would be King.

In seven days he would be back in Tolmirós, the country before him. But for now he was here, with a woman who knew nothing of his life, his people, his duties.

'This is perfect,' she groaned, arching her back so two pert breasts pushed skyward and he shoved his guilt at this deception aside, his guilt at having taken an innocent young woman to bed for his own pleasure, to slake his own needs, knowing it could never be more than this.

She didn't want complications either. They'd been clear on that score. It was this weekend and nothing more. But he was using her, of that he had no doubt. He was using her to rebel, one last time. Using her to avoid the inevitable truth of his life, for one night longer. Using her because right here, in this moment, sleeping with Frankie made him feel human—only human—and not even an inch royal.

He took one of her breasts in his mouth and rolled his tongue over the tight nipple. It budded in his mouth, desperate for his touch, his possession, and he thrust into her depths, wondering if any woman had ever been so perfectly made for a man?

His fingers fisted in her long, silky blonde hair and he pushed her head up to meet his, claiming her lips, kissing her until she whimpered beneath him and the whole of her body was at his command.

Power surged through him at the way this felt, but it was nothing to the power that awaited him, the duty that would soon be at his feet.

For his country and his people, he would turn his back on pleasures such as this, on women such as Frankie, and he would be King.

But not quite yet.

For a few more hours he would simply be Matt, and Frankie would be his…

CHAPTER ONE

Three years later

NEW YORK SPARKLED like a beautiful diorama, all high-rises, bright lights and muted subway noise. He stared down at the glittering city from the balcony of his Manhattan penthouse, breathing in the activity and forcing himself not to remember the last time he'd been in this exact position.

Forcing his eyes to stay trained in the opposite direction of the School of Art, and definitely not allowing himself to remember the woman who had bewitched him and charmed him.

The woman who had given him her innocence, given him her body, and imprinted something of herself in his mind.

Inwardly he groaned, her name just a whisper in his body, a curse too, because he had no business so much as thinking of her, let alone remembering everything about her.

Not when his engagement would be made formal within a month. Not when his future awaited—and duty to his country called to him as loudly as ever. Then, he'd been one week away from assuming the throne, and now he was weeks away from making a marriage commitment.

All of Tolmirós was waiting for its King to finally wed and beget an heir. An heir that would promise stability and the safekeeping of the prosperous nation: all of that was on Matthias's shoulders, as much now as it had been then. He'd run from this fate for as long as he could. His family had died when he was only a teenager and the idea of marrying, having his own children, as though you could so easily recreate what had been lost, pressed against his chest like a weight of stone.

But it was needed; it was necessary. His country required its King to beget an heir, and he needed a wife. A suitable wife, like one of the women his assistant had vetted for him. A woman who would be cultured, polished and appropriate.

His eyes shut and there she was: Frankie. Frankie as she'd been that afternoon they'd met, her clothes paint-splattered, her hair scraped back into a ponytail, her smile contagious. His gut clenched.

His wife—his Queen—would be nothing like Frankie.

What they'd shared went beyond logic and reason—it had been an affair that had rocked him to his core because, after only a matter of hours, he'd known he was in danger of forgetting everything he owed to his people if it meant more time with the woman—she had been like some kind of siren, rising out of the sea, drawing him towards danger unknowingly.

And so he'd done what he was best at: he'd drawn

his heart closed, he'd pushed his emotions deep inside, and he'd walked out on her without a backwards glance.

But now, back in New York, he found himself thinking of her in a way he'd trained himself not to. His dreams he could not control, but his waking mind was as disciplined as the man himself, and he saw no point in dwelling on the past, and particularly not on such a brief event.

Only she was everywhere he looked in this city— the lights that sparkled like the depths of her eyes, the elegance of the high-rises that were tall where she had been short, the nimble alertness, the vivid brightness— and he wondered what it would be like to see her once more. Call it idle curiosity, or simply scratching an itch.

He was a king now, not the man he'd been when they'd first slept together. But his needs were the same. His desires. He stared out at the city and the idea grew.

What harm could come from dipping into the past, just for a night?

'The lighting is beyond perfect,' Frankie enthused, glancing her trained artist's eye over the walls of the midtown gallery. The showing was scheduled for the following day; this was her last chance to make sure everything was absolutely as she wanted it to be.

A *frisson* of excitement ran down her spine.

For years she'd been struggling. Establishing oneself as an artist was no mean feat, and every spare penny she made was funnelled into trying to keep a roof over their heads. It was one thing to be a starving artist when you were footloose and fancy-free—there was even a degree of romance to the notion.

The reality was a lot less enjoyable, particularly with a rapidly growing two-and-a-half-year-old to care for and a mountain of bills that seemed to go on for ever.

But this show…

It could be the game-changer she'd been waiting for.

Two broadsheet newspapers had already sent reviewers to have a pre-show viewing, and the opening night had been advertised across the city. Her fingers, her toes and the hairs on her head remained crossed that she might finally catch her big break into the competitive New York art scene.

'I did think of using small spotlights here.' Charles nodded towards some of her favourite landscapes—sun rising over oceans, but all in abstract oils—gashes of colour scratched over the paper to create the impression of day's dawn. Each picture would be interpreted differently by the spectator, and Frankie liked that. It was her take on each day being what you made of it.

'I like the overheads you've chosen,' she demurred, another shiver running down her spine. Her whole body was a tangle of nerves—and she told herself it was because of the exposure. Not the media exposure—the exposure of herself. Every thought, lost dream, wish, fear, feeling had been captured on these canvases. Even the paintings of Leo, with his stunning crop of black curls, intense grey eyes, so shimmery they were almost silver, lashes that curled precociously and wild. He was her little love, her heart and soul, and his image now hung on the walls of this gallery, waiting to be seen by thousands, she hoped, of viewers.

'The door,' Charles murmured apologetically, in response to a sound that Frankie hadn't even noticed. She was moving closer to the painting she'd done of Leo last fall.

He'd been laughing, collecting dropped leaves from the sidewalk and tossing them into the air with all the enthusiasm a two-year-old boy could muster, and as they'd fallen back to earth he'd watched their progress before crouching down and crunching a new selection into his chubby grip.

His joy had been so euphoric she'd had to capture it. So she'd snapped hundreds of photos from different angles, committing the light to her memory, and then she'd worked late into the night.

And she'd done what she did best: she'd taken a mood, a slice of one of life's moments, and locked it onto a canvas. She'd created a visual secret for the viewer to share in, but only for as long as they looked at her work. It was a moment in time, a moment of her life, and now it was art.

'The opening is tomorrow night, sir, but if you'd like to take a brief look at the collection...'

'I would.'

Two words, so deep, and from a voice so instantly familiar.

A shiver ran down Frankie's spine of a different nature now. It wasn't a shiver of anxiety, nor joyous anticipation, it was one of instant recognition, a tremble of remembrance and a dull thudding ache of loss.

She turned slowly, as if that could somehow unstitch the reality she knew she'd found herself in. But when she looked at Charles, and then the man beside him, all her worlds came crashing down at once.

Matt.

It was him.

And everything came rushing back to her—the way she'd awoken to find him gone, no evidence he'd even slept in the same bed as her, no note, nothing. No way of contacting him, nothing to remember him by except the strange sensation of her body having been made love to, and a desire to feel that sensation again and again.

'Hello, Frances,' he said, his eyes just exactly as she remembered, just exactly like Leo's. How many dreams had she spent painting those eyes? Mixing exactly the right shades of silver, grey and flecks of white to flick, close to the iris? The lashes, with their luxuriant black curls, had occupied much of her artist's mind. How to transpose them onto canvas without looking heavy-handed? They were so thick and glossy that no one would actually believe they really existed.

It had been three years since Frankie had seen this man but, courtesy of her dreams, she remembered him as vividly as if they'd met only the day before.

Oh, how she wanted to drag her eyes down his body, to luxuriate in every inch of him, to remember the strength in his frame, the contradictory gentleness he'd shown when he'd taken possession of her body that first time, when he'd held her in his arms and removed the vestiges of her innocence. How she wanted to give into the temptation to hungrily devour him with her gaze.

With the greatest of efforts, she crossed her arms over her chest and maintained her attention on his face. A face that was watching her with just as much intensity as she was him.

'Matt,' she murmured, proud beyond description when her voice came out steady and cool. 'Are you looking for a piece of art?'

Something seemed to throb between them. A power source that was all its own, that Frankie pushed aside. It wasn't welcome.

'Would you show me your work?' he responded, and it wasn't an answer. It was an invitation, one that was fraught with danger. Belatedly, she recollected that the wall of paintings behind her was of their son and if he looked a little to the left or right he'd see clearly for himself the proof of their weekend together.

'Fine,' she agreed, a little rushed, moving deeper into the gallery, towards another annex. 'But I only have a few minutes.'

At this, she saw Charles frown in her peripheral vision. No wonder he was confused. Without knowing anything about Matt, it was clear that he had enough money to buy everything in the place, probably a million times over. From the fit of his suit to the gleam of his shoes, this was a man who obviously lived very, very comfortably. In normal circumstances, she wouldn't dream of rejecting a potential investor in her work.

But Matt?

Matt who'd crashed into her world, seduced her effortlessly, triumphed over her and gone away again, just as quickly? He was danger, and not for anything would she spend more time with him than she had to.

He's your son's father. Her conscience flared to life and she almost stopped walking, so intense was the realisation, the moral impetus that stabbed into her sides.

'I will take over when Miss Preston leaves.' Charles's offer came from just behind them.

Matt stopped walking, turning to face the other man. 'Miss Preston's company will be sufficient.'

Frankie saw pink bloom in the gallery owner's face and sympathy swelled in her. Charles La Nough's gallery was renowned in New York, and he was used to being met with respect, if not a degree of awe.

To be dismissed in such a way was obviously a new experience.

'I'll call if we need you,' Frankie offered, to soften the blow.

'Very well.' Charles sniffed, turning and disappearing in the direction of the rooms that would eventually lead to the front door.

'You didn't have to be so rude,' she responded, only this time the words were breathy and her pulse was rushing inside her. They were close—just a few feet apart—and she could smell him, she could feel his warmth and her skin was pricking with goosebumps.

Responses she had long since thought dead were stirring to life and demanding indulgence. But she ignored them—such feelings had no place here, or anywhere any more. She tilted her chin defiantly and stared at him. 'And now that he's gone you can tell me exactly what you're doing here. Because I know it's not to buy one of my paintings.'

He regarded her through shuttered eyes. Memory was a funny thing. He'd recollected her in intimate detail over the years, but there were a thousand minute differences now that he stood toe to toe with Frankie Preston. Things his mind hadn't properly written into his memory banks, so that he wanted to hold her still and just *look*.

She remained the most distractingly intriguing woman he'd ever seen, and yet there was no one thing in particular he could ascribe that to. It was *everything* about her—from eyes that were feline in shape and just as green as he remembered, to a nose that had a tiny ski jump at its end and a flurry of pale freckles rushing over its bridge, and lips—*Dio*, those lips.

Pink and pillowy, soft, so that when he'd crushed his mouth to them three years earlier they'd parted on a husky sigh, surrendering to him, welcoming him. His body tightened at the recollection.

Then, she'd been coming home from an art class, carrying a rolled-up canvas in a bag, wearing a pair of paint-splattered jeans and a simple white singlet top, also marked with the signs of her artistic labour. And she'd been so distracted in her own thoughts that she'd walked right into him, smearing a healthy dose of what he'd later discovered to be Cerulean Blue on his suit.

He'd liked her in those clothes—so casual and relaxed. Now, she wore a dress, black with puffy sleeves that just covered her shoulders and a neckline that dipped frustratingly close to her cleavage without revealing even a hint of the generous curves beneath. It fell to her ankles, and she'd teamed it with leather sandals and a bright yellow necklace. It was a more elegant ensemble, but still so very Frankie.

As she was in his mind, anyway.

But wasn't it more than likely that the woman he'd slept with three years earlier was more a creation of his than a real-life, flesh-and-blood woman? Wasn't it more than likely he'd created a fantasy? How well could he have really known her, given that they'd spent so little time together?

'How do you know,' he drawled, considering her question, 'that I am not here to make a purchase?'

She blotted her lips together; they were painted the most fascinating shade of dark pink—as if she'd been feasting on sun-warmed cherries and the natural pigments had stained her mouth.

'Because you're not interested in my art.'

He thought of the piece in his office, the piece he'd bought through a dealer to keep his acquisition at arm's length—the painting Frankie had been working on the day they'd met—and frowned slightly. 'Why would you say that?'

A hint of pink bloomed in her cheeks. 'Well, I remember clearly how well you played me. Pretending interest in my work is how you fooled me then. I won't be so stupid this time around. So what is it that brings you to the gallery, Matt?'

Her use of that name filled him with a confusing

rush of emotions. Shame at having given her only the diminutive of his full name, because surely it proved that he'd set out to deceive her, even from that first moment? Pleasure at the memories it invoked—no other woman had called him that; it was *their* name, it belonged to that weekend, and he would hear it on her lips for ever, calling out to him at the height of her passion.

He wanted her.

Even now, after three years, after walking away from her, he congratulated himself on doing the right thing. He'd been strong in the face of incomprehensible temptation, and he'd done it for his kingdom.

But...

Oh, yes. He wanted her.

Moving slightly closer, just enough to be able to catch a hint of her vanilla perfume, he spoke, his eyes intent when they met hers.

'I am to marry. Soon.'

His words seemed to come to her from a long way away, as though he were shouting from atop a high-rise, and the floor of the gallery lifted in one corner like a rug being shaken, threatening to tip her off the sides of the earth.

I am to marry.

Her stomach rolled with what she told herself must be relief. Because his impending marriage meant she was safe—safe from the flashes of desire that were warming her insides, safe from an insane need to revisit the past even though it was so obviously better left there. How dare she feel like that, when he'd walked out on her without having the decency to leave so much as a note?

'That's nice,' she said, the words not quite as clear and calm as she'd have liked. 'So perhaps you are after a painting after all? A wedding present for your wife?' She spun on her heel, moving deeper into the gallery. 'I have some lovely landscapes I painted out in Massachusetts. Very pretty. Romantic. Floaty.' She was babbling but she couldn't help it.

I am to marry. Soon. His words were running around and around in her mind, ricocheting off the edges of her consciousness.

'Perhaps this piece.' She gestured to a painting of a lake, surrounded by trees on the cusp of losing their leaves, orange and bright, against a beautiful blue sky. Her heart panged as she remembered the day, that slice of life, when she'd taken Leo on their first vacation and they'd toured Paxton and its surroundings.

'Frankie…' His voice was deep and, though he spoke softly, it was with a natural command, a low, throbbing urgency that had her spinning to face him and—damn him—remembering too much of their time together, the way he'd groaned her name as he'd buried his lips at her neck, then lower, teasing her nipples with his tongue.

Only he was so much closer than she'd realised, his large frame right behind her, so when she turned their bodies brushed and it was as though a thousand volts of electricity were being dumped into her system.

She swallowed hard then took a step backwards, but not far enough. It gave her only an inch or so of breathing space and when she inhaled he was there, filling her senses. *He's getting married!*

'What are you doing here?' She didn't bother to hide the emotion in the question. He was a part of her past that hadn't been good. Oh, the weekend itself, sure, but waking up to discover he'd literally walked out on her? To find herself pregnant and have no way of contacting him? The embarrassment of having to hire a detective who even then could discover no trace of this man?

'I...' The word trailed off as he echoed her movement, taking a step forward, closing the distance between them. His expression was tense; his face wore a mask of discontent. Frustration and impatience radiated off him in waves. 'I wished to see you again. Before my wedding.'

She took a moment, letting his statement settle into her mind, and she examined it from all angles. But it made no sense. 'Why?'

His nostrils flared, his eyes narrowed with intent. 'Do you ever think about our time together?'

And the penny dropped and fury lashed at her spine, powerful and fierce, so she jerked her head away from him and bit back a curse her adoptive mother certainly wouldn't have approved of.

'Are you kidding me with this, Matt? You're getting *married* and you're here to walk down memory lane?' She moved away from him, further into the room, her pulse hammering, her heart rushing.

He was watching her with an intensity that almost robbed her of breath. Only she was angry too, angry that he thought he could show up after all this time and ask about that damned weekend…

'Or did you want to do more than walk down memory lane? Tell me you didn't come here for another roll in the hay?' she demanded, crossing her arms over her chest, then wishing she hadn't when his eyes dropped to the swell of her cleavage. Indignation made her go on the attack. 'You can't be so hard up for sex that you're resorting to trawling through lovers from years ago?'

A muscle throbbed low in his jaw as her insult hit its mark. Matt Whatever-his-last-name-was was clearly all macho alpha pride. Her suggestion had riled him. Well, so what? She couldn't care less.

'And no, I *don't* think about that weekend!' she snapped before he could interject. 'So far as I'm concerned, you're just some blip in my rear-view mirror—and if I could take what happened between us back, I would,' she lied, her stomach rolling at the betrayal of their son.

'Oh, really?' he asked softly, words that were dangerous and seductive all at once, his husky accent as spicy and tempting as it had been three years earlier.

'Yes, really.' She glared at him to underscore her point.

'So you don't think about the way it felt when I kissed you here?' She was completely unprepared for his touch—the feather-light caress of a single finger against her jaw, the pulse-point there moving into frantic overdrive as butterflies stormed through her chest.

'No.' The word was slightly uneven.

'Or the way you liked me to touch you here?' and he drew his finger lower, to her décolletage, and then lower still, to the gentle curve of her breast.

Heaven help her, memories were threatening to pull her under, to drown her with their perfection, even when the truth of their situation was disastrous.

Just for a second, she wanted to surrender to those recollections. She wanted to pretend they didn't have a son together and that they were back in time, in that hotel room, just him and her, no consciousness of the outside world.

But it would be an exercise in futility.

'Don't.' She batted his hand away and stepped away from him, anger almost a match for her desire. She rammed her hands against her hips, breathing in hard, wishing there was even the slightest hint of his having been as affected by those needs as she had been. 'It was three years ago,' she whispered. 'You can't just show up after all this time, after disappearing into thin air...'

He watched her from a face that was carefully blanked of emotion, his expression mask-like. 'I had to see you.'

Her heart twisted at those words, at the sense that perhaps he'd found it impossible to forget their night together. Except he'd done exactly that. He'd walked away without a backwards glance. He could have called her at any time in the past three years, but he hadn't. Nothing. Not a blip.

'Well, you've *seen* me,' she said firmly. 'And now I think you should go.'

'You're angry with me.'

'Yes.' She held his gaze, her eyes showing hurt and betrayal. 'I woke up and you were *gone*! You don't think I have a right to be angry?'

A muscle twisted at the base of his firm, square jaw. 'We agreed we would just spend the weekend together.'

'Yes, but that wasn't tacit approval for you to slink out in the middle of the night.'

His eyes narrowed. 'I did *not* slink.' And then, as if bringing himself back to the point, he was calm again, his arrogant face blanked of any emotion once more. 'And it was best for both of us that I left when I did.'

It was strange, really, how she'd been pulling her temper back into place, easing it into the box in which it lived, only to have it explode out of her, writhing free of her grip with a blinding intensity. 'How? How was you disappearing into thin air *best* for me?' she demanded, her voice raised, her face pale.

He sighed as though she were a recalcitrant toddler and his impatience at fraying point. 'My life is complicated.' He spoke without apology, words that were cool and firm and offered no hint of what had truly motivated his departure. 'That weekend was an aberration. In retrospect, I shouldn't have let it happen. I had no business getting involved with someone like you.'

'Someone like me?' she repeated, the words deceptively soft when inside her cells were screeching with indignation. 'But it was fine to sleep with someone like me?'

'You misunderstand my meaning,' he said with a shake of his head. 'And that is my fault.'

'So what is your meaning?'

He spoke slowly, carefully, as though she might not comprehend. 'I wanted you the minute I saw you, Frankie, but I knew it could *never* be more than that weekend. I believe I was upfront about that; I apologise if you expected more from me.' He went to move closer but she bristled, and he stilled. 'There are expectations upon me, expectations as to who I will marry, and you are not the kind of bride I would ever be able to choose.'

She spluttered her interruption. 'I didn't want to *marry* you! I just wanted the courtesy of a goodbye from the man I lost my virginity to. When you crept out of that hotel suite, did you stop to think about what I would think?'

She had the very slight satisfaction of seeing something like remorse briefly glance across his stony features. 'I had to leave. I'm sorry if that hurt you—'

'Hurt me?' She glared at him and shook her head. It had damned near killed her, but she wasn't going to tell him that. 'What *hurts* is your stupidity! Your lack of decency and moral fibre.'

He jerked his face as though she'd slapped him, but she didn't stop.

'You were my first lover.' She lowered her voice. 'Sleeping with you *meant* something to me! And you just left.'

'What would you have had me do, Frankie? Stay and cook you breakfast? Break it to you over scrambled eggs and salmon that I was going to go back to Tolmirós to forget all about you?'

Her stare was withering. 'Only you haven't forgotten me, have you?'

She held her breath, waiting for him to answer, her lips parted.

'No,' he agreed finally. 'But I left because I knew I needed to. I left because I knew what was expected of me.' He expelled a harsh breath, then another, slowly regaining control of himself. 'I didn't come here to upset you, Frankie. I'll go away again.'

And at that, true, dark anger beat in her breast because it simply underscored their power imbalance. He'd come to her and so she was seeing him again, and he'd touched her as though desire was still a current in the room—it was all on his terms. All his timeline, his power, his control. He thought he could leave when it suited him and have that be the end of it.

Well, damn him, he had no right! 'Did you even think about the consequences of that night, Matt? Did you so much as give even a second thought to whether or not I would be able to walk away from what we shared as easily as you did?'

CHAPTER TWO

FOR THE BRIEFEST of moments he misunderstood. Surely, he'd misunderstood.

As the heir to the throne of Tolmirós, Matthias had *never* taken any risks with sex. That weekend had been no different. He'd employed protective measures. He'd been careful, as always.

'I knew there would be no consequences,' he said, shrugging, as though his heart hadn't skidded to a dramatic halt seconds earlier. 'And I truly believed a clean break would be better for you.'

And for himself. He hadn't trusted his willpower to so much as call her, to explain who he was and his reasons for needing to disappear from her life.

'*How* did you know that?'

His frown was infinitesimal. 'Are you saying there was a consequence?'

'A consequence?' she repeated with an arched brow. But her fingers were shaking, a small gesture but one he noted with growing attention. 'Why are we speaking in euphemisms? Ask what you really mean.'

She spoke to him in a way no one in his life had ever

dared, and it was thrilling and dangerous and his whole body resonated with a need to argue with her, just like this. Passions were stirring inside him but he shoved them aside, focusing everything on whatever the hell she was trying to say.

'You are the one who is insinuating there was a complication from our night together.'

'I'm *telling* you your arrogant presumption that you took sufficient measures to protect me from the ramifications of our sleeping together is wrong.'

He narrowed his eyes and her words sprayed around them like fine blades, slicing through the artwork on the walls.

'Are you saying you fell pregnant?' he demanded, his ears screeching with the sound of frantically racing blood. The world stood still; time stopped.

For a moment he imagined that—his child, growing in her belly—and his chest swelled with pride and his heart soared, but pain was right behind, because surely it wasn't possible. His forehead broke out in perspiration at the very idea of his baby. He knew it was inevitable and necessary, but he still needed time to brace himself for that reality—for the idea of another person who shared his blood, a person who could be taken from him at any time.

Rejection was in every line of his body. 'We were careful. *I* was careful. I took precautions, as I always do.'

'Charming!' She crossed her arms over her chest. 'Tell me more about the other women you've had sex with, please.'

He ground his teeth together. He hadn't meant that, and yet it was true. Sexual responsibility was ingrained in Matthias. Anyone in his position would take that seriously.

'What the hell are you saying?' he demanded, all the command his position conferred upon him in those words.

She sucked in a deep breath as though she was steadying herself. 'Fine. Yes. I fell pregnant.' Her words hit him right in the solar plexus, each with the speed and strength of a thousand bullets.

'What?' For the first time in his life, Matthias was utterly lost for words.

When his family had died and a nation in mourning had looked to him, a fifteen-year-old who'd lost his parents and brother, who'd been trapped in a car with them as life had left their bodies, he had known what was expected of him. He'd received the news and wrapped his grief into a small compartment for indulgence at a later date, and he'd shown himself to be strong and reliable: a perfect king-in-waiting.

She lifted her fingertips to the side of her head, rubbing her temples, and fixed him with her ocean-green stare. Her anguish was unmistakable.

'I found out about a month after you left.'

His world was a place that made no sense. There were sharp edges everywhere, and nothing fitted together. 'You were pregnant?'

She pulled a face. 'I just said that.'

His eyes swept shut, his blood raced. 'You should have told me.'

'I *tried*! You were literally impossible to find.'

'No one is impossible to find.'

'Believe me, *you* are. "Matt". That's all I had to go on. The hotel wouldn't give me any information about who'd booked the suite. I had your name and the fact you're from Tolmirós. That's it. I *wanted* to tell you. But trying to find you was like looking for a needle in an enormous haystack.'

And hadn't he planned for it to be this way? A night without complications—that was what they'd shared. Only everything about Frankie had been complicated, including the way she'd cleaved her way into his soul.

'So you made a decision like this on your own?' he fired back, the pain of what he'd lost, what his kingdom had lost, the most important thing in the conversation.

'Decision?' She paled. 'It was hardly a decision.'

'You had an abortion and took from me any chance to even know my child,' he said thickly, his chest tight, his organs squeezing inside him.

She sucked in a loud breath. 'What makes you think I had an abortion?'

He stared at her, the question hanging between them, everything sharp and uncertain now. When he was nine years old he'd run the entire way around the palace, without pausing for even a moment. Up steps, along narrow precipices with frightening glimpses of the city far beneath him, he'd run and he'd run, and when he'd finished he'd collapsed onto the grass and stared at the clouds. His lungs had burned and he'd been conscious of the sting of every cell in his body, as though he was somehow supersonic. He felt that now.

'You're saying…' He stared at her, trying to make sense of this, looking for an explanation and arriving at only one. 'You didn't have an abortion?'

'Of course I didn't.'

Matthias had a rapier-sharp mind, yet he struggled to process her words, to make sense of what she was saying. 'You did not have an abortion?'

'No.'

And something fired inside his mind, a memory, a small recollection that had been unimportant at the time. He spun away from her and stalked through the gallery, through the smaller display spaces that curved towards a larger central room. And he stared at the wall that had framed Frankie when he'd first walked in. He'd been so blindsided by the vision of her initially that he hadn't properly understood the significance of what he was seeing. But now he looked at the paintings—ten of them in total, all of the same little boy—and his blood turned into lava in his veins.

He stared at the paintings and a primal sense of pride and possession firmed inside him. Something else too. Something that made his chest scream and his brow heat—something that made acid coat his insides, as he stared at the boy who was so familiar to him.

Spiro.

He was looking at a version not only of his younger self, but also of his brother. Eyes that had held his, pain and anguish filling them, as life ebbed from him. Eyes that had begged him to help. Eyes that had eventually clouded and died as Matthias watched, helpless, powerless.

For a moment he looked towards the ground, his chest heaving, his pulse like an avalanche, and he breathed in, waiting for the familiar panic to subside.

'This is my son.' More than his son—this was his kin, his blood, his.

He didn't have to turn around to know she was right behind him.

'He's two and a half,' Frankie murmured, the words husky. She cleared her throat audibly. 'His name is Leo.'

Matthias's eyes swept shut as he absorbed this information. Leo. Two and a half. Spiro had been nine when he'd died, the vestiges of his boyish face still in evidence. Cheeks that were rounded like this, and dimpled when he smiled, eyes that sparkled with all his secrets and amusements.

He pushed the memories away, refusing to give into them like this. Only in the middle of the night, when time seemed to slip past the veil of living, when ancient stars with their wisdom and experience whispered that they would listen, did he let his mind remember, did he let his heart hurt.

He turned his attention to the paintings, giving each one in turn the full power of his inspection. Several of the artworks depicted Leo—his son—in a state of play. Laughing as he tossed leaves overhead, his sense of joy and vitality communicated through the paint by Frankie's talented hand. Other paintings were a study of portraiture.

It was the final picture that held him utterly in its thrall.

Leo was staring out of the canvas, his expression

frozen in time, arresting a moment of query. One brow was lifted, his lips were turned into a half-smile. His eyes were grey, like Matthias's—in fact, much of his face was a carbon copy of Matthias's own bearing. But the freckles that ran haphazardly across the bridge of his nose were all Frankie's, as was the defiant amusement that stirred in the boy's features.

Emotions welled inside Matthias, for his own face was only borrowed—first from his father, King Stavros, and it had now been passed onto his own son. What other features and qualities were held by this boy, this small human who was of his own flesh and blood?

His own flesh and blood! An heir! An heir his country was desperate for, an heir he had been poised to marry in order to beget—an heir, already living! An heir, two years old, who he knew nothing about!

'Where is he?' The question was gravelled.

He felt her stiffen—he felt everything in that moment, as though the universe was a series of strings and fibres connected through his body to hers. He turned around, pinning her with a gaze that shimmered like liquid metal.

'Where.' The word was a slowly flying bullet. 'Is.' He took a step closer to her. 'He?'

All the myths upon which he'd been raised, the beliefs of his people as to the power and strength that ran through his veins, a power that was now in his son's veins, propelled him forward. But it was not purely a question of royal lineage and the discovery of an heir. This was an ancient, soul-deep need to meet his son— as a man, as a father.

Alarm resonated from Frankie and until that moment he'd never understood what the term 'mother bear' had been coined for. She was tiny and slight but she looked more than capable of murdering him with her bare hands if he did anything to threaten their child.

'He's outside the city,' she said evasively, her eyes shifting towards the door. Through it was the foyer, and somewhere there the man who ran this gallery. Her fear was evident, and it served little purpose. He was no threat to her, nor their son.

With the discipline he was famed for, Matthias brought his emotions tightly under control. They didn't serve him in that moment. Just like his grief had needed to be contained when his family had been killed, so too did his feelings need to be now.

His whole world had shifted off its axis, and he had to find a way to fix that. To redefine the parameters of his being. An heir was driving his need for marriage and here, it turned out, an heir already existed! There was no option for Matthias but to bring that child home to Tolmirós.

His future shifted before his eyes, and this woman was in it, and their son. All the reasons he'd had for walking away from her still stood, except for this heir. It changed everything.

'I had no idea you were pregnant.'

'Of course you didn't. How could you? You probably walked out as soon as I fell asleep.'

No, he'd waited longer than that. He'd watched her sleep for a while, and thought of his kingdom, the expectations that he would return to Tolmirós and take up his title and all the responsibilities that went with that. Frankie had been a diversion—a distraction. She'd been an indulgence when he'd known he was on the cusp of the life he'd been destined to lead.

Only she'd also been quicksand, and a fast escape had seemed the only solution. The longer he'd lingered, the deeper he'd risked sinking, until escape had no longer been guaranteed.

Besides, he'd comforted himself at the time, he'd made her no promises. He'd told her he was only in the States for the weekend. There were no expectations beyond that. He hadn't broken his word.

'If you'd left your number, I would have called. But you just vanished into thin air. Not even the detective I hired could find you.'

'You hired a detective?' The admission sent sparks through him—sparks of relief and gratitude. Because she hadn't intentionally kept their son a secret. She'd wanted him to be a part of the boy's life. And if he'd known of the child back then? If he'd discovered Frankie's pregnancy?

He would have married her. Her lack of suitability as a royal bride would have been beside the point: his people cared most for the delivery of an heir.

And now he had one.

Every possibility and desire narrowed into one finite realisation. There was only one way forward and the sooner he could convince Frankie of that, the better.

'Yes.' She looked away from him and swallowed visibly, her throat chording before his eyes and his gut clenched as he remembered kissing her there, feeling the fluttering of her racing pulse beneath her fine, soft skin. 'I felt you should know.'

'Indeed.' He dipped his head forward and then, appealing to the sense of justice he knew ran through her passionate veins, 'Will you come for dinner with me?'

Her refusal was imminent but he shook his head to forestall her. 'To discuss our son. You must see how important that is?'

She was tense, her face rigid, her eyes untrusting. But finally she nodded. A tight shift of her head and an even tighter grimace of those cherry-stained lips. 'Fine. But just a quick meal. I told Becky I'd be home by nine.'

'Becky?'

'My downstairs neighbour. She helps out with Leo when I'm working.'

He filed this detail away, and the image it created, of the mother of his child, the mother of the heir to the throne of Tolmirós, a child worth billions of euros, being minded by some random woman in the suburbs of New York.

'A quick meal, then,' he said, giving no indication he was second-guessing her child-minding arrangements.

'Well?' The owner of the gallery appeared from behind the desk, his eyes travelling from Frankie to Matthias. 'Isn't she talented?'

'Exceptionally,' Matthias agreed, and he'd always known that to be the case. 'I will take all of the artworks against that wall.' He gestured through the doorway, to the display that housed the portraits of his son.

'You'll what?' Frankie startled as she looked up at

him, though he couldn't tell if she was surprised or annoyed.

He removed a card from his wallet. 'If you call the number on this card, my valet will arrange payment and delivery.' He nodded curtly and then put a hand in the small of Frankie's back, guiding her towards the front door.

Shock, apparently, held her quiet. But once they emerged onto the Manhattan street, a sultry summer breeze warming the evening, she stopped walking, jerking out of his reach and spinning to face him.

'Why did you do that?'

'You think it strange that I should want paintings of my son?'

She bristled and he understood—she had yet to come to terms with the fact that he was also the boy's parent, that she now had to share their son.

Not only that—he couldn't have paintings of his child, the heir to his throne, for sale in some gallery in New York. It wasn't how things were done.

'No,' she admitted grudgingly, and the emotion of this situation was taking its toll on her. The strength and defiance she carried in her eyes were draining from her. Wariness took their place.

'Come on.' He gestured towards the jet-black SUV that was parked in front of the gallery. Darkly tinted windows concealed his driver and security detail from sight but, as they approached, Zeno stepped out, opening the rear doors with a low bow.

Frankie caught it, her eyes narrowing at the gesture of deference. It was so much a part of Matthias's day that he barely noticed the respect with which he was treated. Seeing it through Frankie's eyes though, he understood. It was confronting and unusual.

'You know, I never even had your surname,' she murmured as she slid into the white leather interior of the car—her skin was so pale now it matched the seats.

There was so much he wanted to ask about that. Would she have given their child his name if she'd known it? The idea of his son being raised as anything other than a Vasilliás filled him with a dark frustration.

He wanted to ask her this, and so much more, but not even in front of his most trusted servants would he yet broach the subject of his heir.

With a single finger lifted to his mouth, he signalled silence and then settled back into the car himself, brooding over this turn of events and what they would mean for the marriage he had intended to make.

'I presumed you meant dinner at a restaurant,' she said as the car pulled up to a steel monolith on United Nations Plaza. The drive had been conducted in absolute silence, except for when the car drew to a stop and he'd spoken to his driver in that language of his, all husky and deep, so her pulse had fired up and her stomach had churned and feelings that deserved to stay buried deep in the past flashed in her gut, making her nerveendings quiver and her pulse fire chaotically against the fine walls of her veins.

'Restaurants are not private enough.'

'You can't speak quietly in a restaurant?'

'Believe me, Frankie, this is better.' His look was

loaded with intensity and there was a plea in the depth
of his gaze as well, begging her to simply agree with
him on this occasion. There was a part of her, a childish, silly part, that wanted to refuse—to tell him it didn't
suit her. He'd disappeared into thin air and she'd tried
so hard to find him, to tell him he was a father. And
now? Everything was on his terms. She wanted to rebel
against that, but loyalty to their son kept her quiet. All
along, she'd wanted what was best for Leo. She'd spent
all her life feeling rejected and unwanted by her biological parents, and she had wept for any idea that Leo
might feel the same! That Leo might grow up believing
his father hadn't wanted him.

'Fine,' she agreed heavily. 'But I really can't stay long.'

'This is not a conversation to be rushed.' He stepped
out of the car and she followed. He placed a hand on
her elbow, guiding her through the building's sliding
glass doors. The lifts were waiting, a security guard
to one side.

She hadn't noticed this degree of staff with him back
then. There hadn't been anyone except a driver, and
she'd never really questioned that. It was obvious that he
had money—but this was a whole new degree of wealth.

'Have you had some kind of death threat or something?' she muttered as the doors of the lift snapped
closed behind them.

The look he sent her was half-rueful, half-impatient;
he said nothing. But when the lift doors opened into the
foyer of what could only be described as a sky palace,
he urged her into the space and then held a hand up to
still the guard.

More words, spoken in his own tongue, and then the guard bowed low and slipped back into the lift, leaving them alone.

She swallowed at that thought—being alone with him—distracting herself by studying the over-the-top luxury of this penthouse. It wasn't just the polished timber floors, double height ceilings, expensive designer furnishings and crystal chandeliers that created the impression of total glamour. It was the views of the Manhattan skyline—the Chrysler Building, the Empire State, Central Park—it all spread before her like a pop-up book of New York city.

Large sliding glass doors opened out onto a deck, beyond which there was a pool, set against a glass rail. She imagined swimming in it would feel a little like floating, high above the city.

The contrasts between her own modest apartment in Queens and this insanely beautiful penthouse were too ridiculous to enumerate.

'Matt,' she sighed, turning to face him, not even sure what she wanted to say. He was watching her with a look of dark concentration.

'My name,' he said quietly, 'is Matthias Vasilliás.'

It was perfect for this man—as soon as he gave her the full version of his name it resonated inside her, like the banging of a drum. *Matt* was too pedestrian for someone like him. He was exotic and unusual.

'Fine.' She nodded curtly, pleased when the word sounded vaguely dismissive. 'Matthias.'

At this, his eyes flashed with something she couldn't comprehend. 'You have not heard of me?'

Something like an alarm bell began to ring inside Frankie's mind. 'Should I have?'

His lips twisted in a sardonic smile. 'No.'

But it sounded like judgement rather than offence, and she bristled. 'So? What gives?' Her frown deepened. 'What's with all the security?'

He sighed heavily. 'This is a light protection detail.' He shrugged. 'At home, there are many more guards.'

'Why? I don't get it. Are you some kind of celebrity or something?'

'You could say that.'

He moved into the kitchen and pulled out a bottle of wine. Her stomach rolled at the memories of the wine they'd shared that night—only a few sips, but it had been the nicest she'd ever tasted. He poured her a glass and walked around to her; she took it on autopilot.

'What's going on, Matt—Matthias?'

His eyes narrowed and she wondered if the sound of his full name on her lips was as strange for him as it was for her. Matt had suited him, but Matthias suited him better. She liked the taste of those exotic syllables on the tip of her tongue.

'My family was killed in an accident many years ago. When I was a boy of fifteen.' He spoke matter-of-factly, so it was impossible for Frankie to know how those deaths had affected him. She could imagine, though.

'I'm sorry,' she murmured crisply, wishing she didn't feel sympathy for him. Wishing she didn't feel *anything* for him.

His lips twisted in acknowledgement. 'It was a long time ago.'

'I'm sure it still hurts.'

'I have become used to being alone.' He brushed her concern aside. 'My father's brother took on many of the responsibilities of my father. At fifteen, I was too young.'

'What responsibilities?' she asked.

'Shortly after their deaths, it was decided that on my thirtieth birthday I would assume my role.' He pinpointed her with his gaze, but he was obviously back in time, reflecting on the past. 'One week before I turned thirty, I met you. I was only in New York for the weekend. One of my last chances to travel as myself, without this degree of…company.' His expression shifted.

'What did your parents do?'

But this wasn't a conversation with questions and answers. It was a monologue. An unburdening of himself, and it was an explanation she'd wanted for such a long time that she didn't even particularly mind.

'I shouldn't have got involved with you, but you were so… I cannot explain it. I saw you, and I wanted you.' He stared at her, his eyes glinting like steel, and her heart was ice in her chest. It had been that simple for him. He'd seen her. He'd wanted her. And so he'd had her.

'I knew it would only ever be a brief affair.'

Her throat constricted with those words, damning what they'd been to such a cynical seduction. 'Yet you did it anyway?'

He was quiet.

'Did you think about how I'd feel?'

'No.' He swept his eyes shut. 'I told myself you were

just like me—looking for a weekend of pleasure. Casual, easy sex.'

'I think the term "casual sex" is oxymoronic,' she said stiffly, turning away from him so she didn't see the way his expression shifted, the way a fierce blade of possession pressed into him.

'If I had known you were a virgin…'

'I didn't lie to you intentionally,' she muttered. 'I just got caught up in how I felt. It was all so overwhelming.'

He dipped his head forward in silent concession. 'It is in the past,' he said. 'What I'm interested in dealing with is our future.'

And here it was. The custody discussion she'd been dreading. And as the days had turned into months and her status as a single mother had been firmly established, she'd come to accept that it was a conversation she'd never need to have. Now, though, faced with the father of her baby, she had no interest in denying him his right to see their child. To be a part of his life. Even when his admission that he'd gone into their affair expecting it to be 'casual sex' had cut her deep inside.

'After I left you, I went back to Tolmirós and took up the position that was my birthright.'

She frowned. 'Just what kind of family business are you in?'

His smile was more like a grimace. 'It is not a business, Frankie. My name is Matthias Vasilliás and I am the King of Tolmirós.'

CHAPTER THREE

'I'M SORRY.' SHE blinked slowly. 'I thought you just said you were...' She laughed, a brittle sound of disbelief. 'I mean, is this some kind of joke?'

But she looked around the penthouse with new eyes, seeing the degree of luxury and wealth as if for the first time, understanding how uniquely positioned a person would have to be to enjoy this kind of residence. And it wasn't just this ludicrously expensive apartment—how much would something like this even cost? More than she could imagine, that was for sure. And she saw *everything* through the veil of his words and her stomach dropped and her knees shook. Because it was *so* obvious now.

Even then, staying at a hotel, he'd been so *different* to anyone she'd ever known. He'd spoken to her of ancient myths and he'd weaved magic into her being.

He'd been totally unique. A king.

'It's no joke. That weekend with you was my way of trying to ignore the reality of how my life was about to change, of pretending I wasn't about to take the throne and the mantle of King. But I do not believe in hiding,

Frankie. And so I left you in order to return to my country, my people, and my role as ruler.'

His words came to her from very far away.

He was a king.

Which meant… Oh, God. She reached behind her for the sofa, dropping down into it with a thud and drinking her wine as though it were a lifeline.

'Yes,' he agreed, moving closer to her, the word drawn from deep in his throat. 'Our son is my heir. He is a prince, Frankie.'

'But…he's not… We weren't married.' She clutched at straws desperately. 'So doesn't that mean he can't be your heir?'

His expression darkened and he took a moment to answer. 'It complicates matters,' he agreed eventually, with a shrug. 'But nothing changes the fact he is the future of my people.'

She swallowed, his certainty formidable.

'Do you remember the Myth of Elektus?'

She swayed a little, the words he'd spoken that night burned into her memories. 'No,' she lied huskily, staring out at New York.

'My family has ruled Tolmirós for over a millennium. Our line remains unbroken. Wars and famines consumed neighbouring countries but, within the borders of Tolmirós, life has been prosperous and stable. The myth of our First Ruler is one my people hold in their hearts, even now. It is believed that my family's lineage is at the root of Tolmirós's wealth and happiness. Leo is *not* simply a boy—he is the fulfilment of a myth and ruling Tolmirós is his destiny, as much as it was mine.'

The magic he'd wound around her heart was weaving into her soul once more, and her beautiful child, who *was* so kingly, even as a child, began to pull away from her as she saw him as a figure of the fabric of this faraway country.

But he wasn't only the heir to Tolmirós's throne: he was her son. A child she had grown in her belly and nursed through fevers and helped to take his first step. He was a child she'd read to every night of his life, played ball with, lain beside when night terrors had caused him to cry out.

'My people need him to come home, Frankie. He is part of that myth—he is our future.'

Her eyes swept shut on a wave of desolation. 'You speak of your people, and you speak of his destiny. These are the words of a king, not a father.' She turned to face him. 'How can you not care about him as your son? He is a little boy and for two and a half years he has existed and all you care about is his destiny to rule a country he hasn't even heard of. You haven't asked me a single thing about him!'

His eyes glittered at the truth of her accusation. 'You think I am not burning to know *every single detail* about my son? You think I am not desperate to meet him and hold him to me, and look into his face and understand him? Of course I am. But first I must secure your understanding for what will happen next. We must move quickly if we are to control this.'

'Control what?'

He expelled an impatient breath and his nostrils flared.

'Our marriage.'

'Marriage?' She paled visibly. 'I'm not marrying *you*!'

'With respect, Frankie, that decision was taken out of our hands the minute you conceived Leo.'

'That's not how I see it.'

'Then let me be clear: there is no reality where I will not be raising my son as my son and heir.'

'Fine. Be his father. Even let him be the heir to your damned country—'

Matthias's expression darkened.

'But don't think you can show up after three years and try to take over our lives. Whatever we shared that night, it was fleeting. Meaningless. Just like you said. And it's over. You're just some guy I frankly wish I'd never met.'

His cheekbones were slashed a dark red. 'That may be the case, but we *did* meet. We slept together and now we have a son. And I cannot ignore that. We must marry, Frankie. Surely you can see it's the only way?'

She drew in a shaking breath at the finality of that, and fear trembled inside her breast.

'No.'

'No?' he repeated, and then laughed, a harsh sound of disbelief. 'You cannot simply say "no" to me.'

'Because you're a king?'

His eyes narrowed watchfully. 'Because I am his father, and I will fight you with every breath in my body to bring him home.'

'He *is* home!'

'He is the heir of Tolmirós and he belongs in the palace.'

'With you?'

'And you. You'll be my wife, the Queen of a prosperous, happy country. It's not like I'm asking you to give him up. Nor to move somewhere unpleasant. You wouldn't even have to live with me—I have many palaces; you could choose which you wanted to reside in. Your life will be significantly improved.'

'How can you say that? I'd be married to you.'

'And?'

'I hardly even know you!' The words flew from her mouth and her body immediately contradicted them. Her body knew his well. So well. Even now, dressed as he was, she saw him naked. She saw his broad, muscular chest, his swarthy tan, his wide shoulders, and her insides slicked with moist heat as—out of nowhere—she remembered the way he'd possessed her utterly and completely.

'We will get to know each other enough.' He shrugged. 'Enough to raise a family together, enough to be a good King and Queen.'

He spoke dispassionately, calmly, but the words he spoke, the images they made, filled her with a warm, tingling sense in her gut. 'It's that easy for you?'

'I've never expected any differently.'

'Wait a second. You told me tonight that you're engaged. So what's your fiancée going to say about this?'

'There is no such person. I haven't yet selected a bride.'

Frankie felt as if her head was about to explode. '"Selected" a bride?' She rolled her eyes. 'You make it sound like shuffling a deck of cards and drawing one at random.'

'It is far from a random process,' he said with a shake of his head. 'Each of the women have been shortlisted because of their suitability to be my wife.'

'So go back to your damned country and marry one of them.'

He swept his heated gaze over her body, and goose-bumps spread where his eyes moved.

'Think it through,' he said finally. 'What happens if I do as you say—if I return to Tolmirós and marry another woman. She becomes my Queen, and Leo is still my son. *Our* son, mine and my wife's. I will fight for custody of him and, Frankie, I will win.' A shiver ran down her spine at his certainty, because she knew he was right. She knew the danger here, for her. 'I will win, and I will raise him. Wouldn't you prefer to avoid an ugly custody dispute, a public battle that you would surely lose? Wouldn't you prefer to accept this and simply agree to marry me?'

'*Simply?*' There was nothing simple about it. 'I would *prefer* you to go right away again.'

He made a small sound—it might have been a laugh, but there was absolutely no humour in it. 'No matter what we might wish, this is the reality we find ourselves in. I have a son. An heir. And I must bring him home. Surely you can see that?'

The city twinkled like a thousand gems against black velvet. She swallowed, her eyes running frantically over the vista as her brain tried to fumble its way to an alternative. 'But marriage is so...'

'Yes?'

'It's so much. Too much.' She spun back to face him, and her heart thudded in her chest. Marriage to this man? Impossible. He had embodied so many fantasies in her mind but, over time, the lust which might have become love, given the proper treatment, had instead turned to resentment.

He'd disappeared into thin air, and she'd made her peace with that.

Now? To expect her just to marry him?

'Why? People do it all the time,' he said simply, moving across the room and pouring a generous amount of Scotch into two tumblers. He carried one over to her and, despite the fact she didn't drink often and the wine had already made her brain fuzzy, she took it as if on autopilot.

'Do what all the time?' Her mind was still fumbling for something to offer that might appease him.

'Get married because it makes sense.'

Now it was Frankie's turn to make a strangled sound. Not a laugh, not a sob—just a noise driven by emotions emanating from deep in her throat. 'People get married because they are in love,' she contradicted forcefully. 'Because they can't bear to spend their lives apart. People get married because they are full of optimism and hope, because they have met the one person on earth whom they can't live without.'

She spoke the words with passion, from deep within her soul; they were words that meant the world to her.

Words by which she lived. But each word seemed to have the effect of making Matthias withdraw from her. His handsome face tightened until his features were stern and his eyes flinted like coal.

'A fantasist's notion,' he said at length. 'And not what I'm offering.'

It was such an insult that she let out a sigh of impatience. 'It's not what I'm asking for—not from you, anyway.' She ignored the strange thumping in the region of her heart. 'I'm explaining that marriage *means* something.'

'Why?' He took a step closer to her, his eyes so focused on her they were like a force, holding her to the spot.

She frowned. 'What do you mean?'

'Why can it not just be that it makes sense?'

'Making sense,' Frankie said with a shake of her head, trying to break free of the power his gaze had over her ability to think straight, 'would be us working out how we're going to do this.' It hurt to think of sharing Leo, but she pushed those feelings aside. This was about Leo, not her. 'You *are* his father, and it was always my wish that you'd be involved in his life. I can bring him to Tolmirós for a visit, to start with, and we can allow him to gradually adjust to the idea of being the heir to your throne. Over time, he might even choose to spend more time over there, with you. And of course you can see him when you're in New York.' Yes. That all made perfect sense. She nodded somewhat stiffly, as though she'd ordered a box neatly into shape. 'There's definitely no need for us to get married.'

'I say there is a need,' he contradicted almost instantly. His voice was calm but there was an intensity in his gaze. 'And within the month.'

'A month?' Her jaw dropped, her stomach swooped and spun.

'Or sooner, if possible. We must act swiftly. There is much you need to learn on the ways of my people. Much Leo will have to learn too.'

'Hang on.' She lifted her hand, pressing it into the air between them as though it might put an end to this ridiculous conversation. 'You can't talk like it's a foregone conclusion that I'll marry you! You've suggested it and I've said, "Absolutely not". You can't just ride roughshod over me.'

His eyes narrowed almost imperceptibly. 'Do you think not?'

'*Definitely* not. Unless you think I'm not a sentient person, capable of making my own decisions?'

'On the contrary. I think you are very capable of that—which is why I'll expect you to make the right one. But be assured, Frankie, regardless of what you think and feel, I have no intention of leaving this country without my son. It is obviously better for everyone if you come with him as my fiancée.'

She sucked in a breath as the truth of what he was saying settled around her. 'You're actually threatening to take him away from me?'

'I'm asking you to marry me.'

Her eyes swept shut. 'Telling me, more like.' When she blinked her eyes open he was closer, so close her palm was almost touching his chest.

'I'm asking you,' he insisted, almost gentle, almost as though he understood her fear and wanted to ease it. 'I'm asking you to see sense. I'm asking you not to put me in a position where I have to fight you for our child.'

Fear lanced her breast because she didn't doubt the sincerity of his words, nor that he had the ability to follow through. She had some savings, but not a lot. Her adoptive parents were comfortable but by no means wealthy. Not in a million years would she be able to afford a lawyer of the calibre necessary to stave off this man's determination. Would he even need a lawyer? Or would he have some kind of diplomatic privilege, given he was King?

'You're such a bastard,' she said, stepping backwards. It was a mistake; the window was behind her. Ice-cold against her back, and rather like a vice clamping her to the spot.

'I am the father to a two-year-old. A little boy I didn't know about even three hours ago. Do you think wanting to raise him is truly unreasonable?'

'Raise him, no. Marry me? Yes.'

'I want this as little as you do, Frankie.' He expelled a sigh and shook his head. 'That is not completely true, in fact. I still want you. I came here tonight because I was thinking of our weekend together and I wished to take you to bed once more.'

She bit down on her tongue to stop a curse from flying from her lips. 'How dare you?' The words were numbed by shock. 'After all these years? After the way you slept with me and then disappeared into thin air?

You thought you could just turn up and have me fall at your feet?'

'You did once before,' he pointed out with insufferable arrogance.

Her fingertips itched with a violent impulse to slap him. 'I didn't know you then!'

'And you don't know me now,' he continued, moving closer, speaking with a softness that was imbued with reasonable, rational intent. It was like a magic spell being cast. His proximity was enough to make her pulse thready and her cheeks glow pink.

But she hated him for the ease with which he could affect her and she did her best to hide any sign that she so much as noticed his proximity.

'You don't know that I am a man who has won almost every battle he's fought. You don't know, perhaps, that I am a man accustomed to getting everything I want, when I want it. You do not know that I have the might of ten armies at my back, the wealth of a nation at my feet, and the heart of a warrior in my body.'

Another step closer and his fingertips lifted to press lightly against her cheek. His eyes held hers, like granite locking her to the window.

'You think I don't know you get what you want?' she returned, pleased when the words came out cool and almost derisive. 'You wanted me that weekend and look how that turned out.'

It was the wrong thing to say. Memories of their sensual, delicious time together punctuated the present, and she was falling into the past. With his body so close, so hard and broad, a random impulse to push onto her tiptoes and find his earlobe with her lips, to wobble it between her teeth before moving to his stubbled jaw and finally those wide, curving lips, made breathing almost impossible.

They were perfect lips, she thought distractedly, her artist's mind working overtime as they studied the sculptured feature.

'You are not seeing anyone else.' It was a statement rather than a question, and his certainty was an insult.

'Why do you say that?' she asked, a little less steadily now.

There was something enigmatic and dangerous in his gaze, something that spoke of promises and need. Something that stilled her heart and warmed her skin. 'You do not react to me like a woman who's in love with another man.'

She sucked in a breath; it didn't reach her lungs. 'What's that supposed to mean?'

His smile was sardonic. 'You look at me with eyes that are hungry for what we shared. You tremble now because I am close to you.' He dropped his fingertips to the pulse point at the base of her neck and she cursed her body's traitorous reaction. 'You do not wish to marry me, Frankie, but you want to be with me again, almost more than you want your next breath.'

Oh, God, it was true, but it was wrong! And there was a difference between animal instincts and intelligent consideration—there was no way she'd be stupid enough to fall prey to his virile, sensual pull. Not again. Only she was already falling, wasn't she? Being drawn into his seductive, tantalising web...

'No,' she denied flatly, moving sideways, proud of herself for putting distance between them, for dismissing him with such apparent ease. If only her knees weren't weak and her nipples weren't throbbing against the lace of her bra. 'And the fact I'm single doesn't mean I'm up for this stupid idea. I'm not marrying you.'

He turned his back on her. His spine was rigid, his shoulders tight in his muscular frame. He paced across the room, reminding her of a prowling animal, some kind of Saharan beast, all lean and strong.

She watched him, her body shivering, her mind struggling to make sense of anything.

'What choice do we have?' He kept his back to her and thrust his hands into his pockets. He was looking out at the city, staring at the view, and his voice had a bleakness to it that reached inside her and filled Frankie with despair.

She followed his gaze; nothing seemed to shine now.

'What choice do I have?' he repeated. 'I have a son. He is a prince, and the fate of my country is on his shoulders. I must bring him home. I owe it… I owe it to my people,' he said firmly. He moved one hand from his pocket to his head, driving his fingers through his dark hair, then turning to face her again. 'And you owe it to Leo, Frankie.' His eyes held hers and there was earnestness and honesty in his expression. 'You want to raise him with me, don't you?'

Her chest tightened because he was right. 'I want to raise a son who is happy and well-adjusted,' she said finally. 'Who has two parents who love him. That doesn't mean we have to marry…'

'When we were together, back then, you told me of your upbringing,' he said with a soft strength in his voice. 'You told me of weekends spent hiking in the summer and playing board games in the winter, reading around the fire, cooking together. You told me how you'd longed for a sister or brother because you wanted a bigger family—lots of noise and happiness. You told me your family meant everything to you. Would you deprive our son of that?'

She stared at him, aghast and hurting, because, damn him, he was right. Everything he'd repeated was exactly as she felt, as she'd always felt, ever since she'd known the first sting of rejection. Since she'd understood that adoption often went hand in hand with abandonment— for the two parents who had chosen to raise her, there were two who had chosen to lose her, to give her away.

She'd seen everything through a prism of that abandonment, never taking family time for granted, seeing it with gratitude because she had feared her adoptive parents' love, once given, might also be taken away again.

Her eyes swept shut and, instead of speaking, she made a strangled noise, deep in her throat.

His eyes swept over her beautiful face and, seeing her surrender, he pushed home his advantage. 'Marry me because our son deserves that of us. You and I slept together, we made a baby together. From the moment of his conception, this stopped being about you and me, and what we both want. We have an obligation to act in his best interests.'

More sense. More words that she agreed with, and suddenly the pull towards marriage was an inevitable force. She knew she would agree—she had to—but she wasn't ready to show him that just yet.

'It's too much,' she whispered, lifting her eyelids and staring at him with confusion and uncertainty. 'Marrying you, even if you were just a normal man, would be…ridiculous. But you're a king and I'm the last person on earth who wants to be…who's suitable to be… I wouldn't be any good at it.'

'First and foremost, you will be my wife, and the mother to my children. Your duties as Queen will not need to be onerous.' He softened his expression. 'In any event, I think you are underselling yourself.'

But she heard nothing after one simple word. 'Children? As in, plural?'

'Of course. One is not enough.' The words were staccato, like little nails being slammed into her sides. Something deep rumbled in his features, a worry that seemed to arrest him deep inside.

But she shook her head, unable to imagine having more children with this man. 'I don't want more children.'

'You do not like being a mother?' he prompted.

'Of course I do. I love Leo. And if I could lay an egg and have four more children, then I would. But, unfortunately, to give you more precious *heirs* I'd need to… we'd need to…'

'Yes?' he drawled, and she had the distinct impression he was enjoying her discomfort.

'Oh, shut up,' she snapped, lifting her fingertips to her temples and massaging them.

'We are getting married,' he said, and apparently her

acquiescence was now a point of fact. 'Do you think the question of sex is one we won't need to address?'

His ability to be so calm in the face of such an intimate conversation infuriated her.

'*If* I were to marry you,' she snapped, resenting his confidence as to her agreement, 'sex wouldn't be a part of our arrangement.'

He laughed. 'Oh, really?'

'Yes, really. And it's not funny! Sex should *mean* something, just like marriage should *mean* something. You're laughing like I'm saying something stupid and I'm not—the way I feel is perfectly normal.'

'You are naïve,' he said with a shake of his head. 'Like the innocent virgin you were three years ago. Sex is a biological function—two bodies enjoying one another: pleasure for pleasure's sake. Marriage is an alliance—a mutually beneficial arrangement. Even those who dress it up as "soulmates" and "love" know it for what it really is, deep down.'

'And what's that?' she demanded.

'Convenience. Companionship. Sex.'

Her cheeks flamed pink. 'How in the hell did you get to be so cynical?' she demanded.

'I am more realist than cynic.' He shrugged insouciantly. 'You will grow up and see things as they really are one day, Frankie.'

'I hope not.'

'Don't be so glum,' he cautioned and, without her realising it, he'd crossed the room and was standing right in front of her. His eyes bored into hers and everything in the room seemed to slow down, to stammer to a stop.

She stared up at him, her heart racing, her mouth dry, her eyes roaming his face hungrily. 'You will enjoy certain aspects of being my wife.'

She swallowed in an attempt to bring moisture back to her mouth. 'You're wrong.'

He laughed, a dry sound, and swooped his head down, to claim her mouth with his. 'When it comes to women and sex, Frankie, I'm never wrong.'

Her pulse hammered in her ears and her body went into overdrive, her nerve-endings tingling, her heart throbbing. She wanted to resist him. God, she wanted to make a point. She wanted to push him away. But with her dying breath, with every fibre of her being, she wanted this more. She lifted her hands, burying them in his shirt, her senses noting everything about him— his warmth, his strength, his masculine fragrance, his closeness, his hardness, his very *him*-ness. Memories of how it had been before flashed through her and she whimpered, low in her throat, when one of his hands moved behind her, cupping her bottom and pulling her forward, pressing her to his arousal until she made a groaning sound, tilting her head back to give him better access to her mouth.

And he dominated her with his kiss, his mouth making a mockery of her objections, his lips showing her how completely he could force her surrender, how quickly he could crumble all her reserves, how quickly he could turn her into trembling putty in his arms.

How little, in that moment, she minded.

He lifted his head, pulling away from her, his breathing roughened by passion, as her own was. 'I have no intention of making your life difficult or unpleasant, Frankie. Through the days, you'll barely know I exist.'

Her pulse was still hammering inside her and her body was weak with desire. When she spoke, the words were faint, breathy. 'And at night?'

'At night,' he promised, lifting his hand and stroking his thumb across her cheek, 'you won't be able to exist without me.'

Matthias stared at his child and inside him it felt as if an anvil were colliding with his ribcage.

The little boy was the spitting image of Spiro, just as the painting had made him appear.

'Hello.' He crouched down so he could look into Leo's face. 'You must be Leo.'

Leo nodded thoughtfully. 'Yes. I am Leo.'

Matthias couldn't smile. He felt only pain, like acid gushing through his veins. How much of this boy's life had he missed? How much was there about him he didn't know?

'We are going to go on an adventure,' he said, standing, glaring at Frankie with all the rage he felt in that moment. The night before, he'd wanted to make love to her until she was incoherent, crying his name at the top of her voice. Now? He felt nothing but rage. Rage at what she'd denied him. Rage at what she'd enjoyed while he'd been none the wiser.

'Come, Leo,' he said, the words carefully muted of harsh inflection even when his eyes conveyed his mood just fine. 'We are going on an adventure together.'

CHAPTER FOUR

HER STOMACH SWOOPED as the plane came in low over the Mediterranean, but Frankie knew it had less to do with the private jet's descent and more to do with the man sitting opposite her. In the incredible luxury of this plane, surrounded by white leather furniture, chandeliers, servants dressed in white and gold uniforms, Matthias still stood out. He was imposing.

Regal.

Grand.

Intimidating.

And he was to be her husband.

Thoughts of their kiss, with her back pressed against a wall literally and metaphorically, flooded her mind and her temperature spiked as remembered pleasures deepened inside her.

The ocean glistened beneath them like a beautiful mirage, dark blue from up here, and dozens of little islands dotted in the middle of it. Each was surrounded by a ring of turquoise water and an edge of crisp white sand.

'That is Tolmirós,' he said conversationally, and it

was the first he'd spoken to her all flight. The silence had been deafening, but Frankie had been preoccupied enough wondering just how the hell she'd found herself being spirited away to this man's kingdom—having agreed, at last, to be his wife!

'Which one?'

He eyed her thoughtfully for a moment and her heart rate notched up a gear. 'All of them. Tolmirós is made up of forty-two islands. Some are small, some are large. Like Epikanas,' he said, reaching across and pointing to an island in the distance.

She looked in the direction he was indicating, trying to ignore the fact that he was so close to her now, so close she could breathe in his woody masculine fragrance. When he'd kissed her, it had been as though nothing else mattered. Not the past, not the future—nothing.

'Epikanas,' she repeated.

'Good.' He nodded his approval and the smile that spread across his face warmed her from the inside out. 'You pronounced that perfectly. You will have a language tutor to help you learn how to speak our language.' He sat back in his seat and she told herself she was glad. The plane moved lower, bumping a little as it pushed through some turbulence. 'Epikanas is the main island—my palace is there, my government centre, the main business hub, our largest city. It is where we will live, most of the time.'

She nodded distractedly, turning in her seat to face him, then wishing she hadn't when she found him watching her intently. She skidded her eyes away again, to the seat across the aisle. It had been put into full recline, forming a bed, and Leo was fast asleep, sprawled lengthways.

She watched him sleep and her heart clenched because she knew, risky though this was for her, she was doing the right thing for Leo. If there was any way she could give her son the security of a family, she was going to do it. Her eyes swept shut for a moment as the single memory she possessed of her birth mother filtered to the top of her mind. It was vague. An impression of a faded yellow armchair, sunlight streaming in through a window, curtains blowing in the slight breeze, and the sound of tapping. Her mother had lifted her, hugged her, smelling like lemons and soap.

Then the memory was gone again, like the parents who hadn't wanted her. No matter how hard she tried to catch it, to unpick it and see more of her early childhood, there was nothing.

Determination fired through her spine.

Leo would never feel like she had; he'd never know that sting of rejection. He'd never know the burden of that loss. Unknowingly, she tilted her chin in a gesture of defiance, her eyes glinting with determination. For her son, she would make this work.

'This,' he said, as if following the direction of her thoughts, 'that we are flying over now is Port Kalamathi,' he said. 'The island used to be an important stronghold in our naval operations. Now, it is home to the best school in Tolmirós. It is here that Leo will go, when he is old enough.'

She looked out of her window at the island that was

just a swirling mix of green and turquoise. In the centre there were buildings—ancient-looking, with lots of gardens and lawns. She supposed that, so far as schools went, the location was excellent. But wasn't it too far from the palace?

She gnawed on her lower lip and pushed that question aside. Their son was two years old: they could cross that bridge when they came to it. It would be years away. She had more immediate concerns to address.

'What happens next?' she asked, sitting back in her seat, clasping her hands in her lap in a gesture that she hoped made her look calm and confident.

He nodded, apparently relieved she was prepared to discuss things rationally. 'My security has kept the press away from the airport. Usually there are photographers on hand when my plane comes in,' he said.

'But not now?'

'No, not now.' He stared into her eyes and her mouth was drier than the Arizona desert. 'Now, there will be just my drivers and security personnel.'

'Do you have security personnel with you often?'

'Always,' he agreed.

'You didn't that weekend.'

'That weekend, I was still a prince.' His look was one of self-derision. 'I was still a boy, running from my destiny.'

She regarded him thoughtfully. 'You said your uncle was King until you turned thirty?'

'Not King, no.' He shook his head. 'Ancient rules govern the line of succession. My uncle was a *prosorinós*. A sort of caretaker for the throne.'

'What if you'd died too?' she asked, and then heat flushed her face as she realised how insensitive the question sounded.

He didn't seem to mind though. He considered it carefully. 'Then, yes, my uncle would have been King.'

She tilted her head to the side. 'I'm sure I heard once that the legal guardian of an heir couldn't assume that heir's title—lest self-interest lead them to murderous deeds.'

He arched a brow. 'True. And it is the same in Tolmirós. My uncle was not my legal guardian. In fact, I was prevented from seeing him more than once or twice a year during that time.'

She absorbed these words, turning them over in her mind before saying with a small frown, 'But he was your only surviving family? No cousins? Aunt?'

'No. He never married.' His expression shifted.

'And you didn't get to see him?'

He shrugged, as though it barely mattered. 'It is the way it had to be.'

She was inwardly appalled. 'Then who raised you?'

'I was fifteen when my family died,' he said dismissively. 'I had already been "raised".'

'You think you were a grown man at that age?' Her heart hurt for the teenager he'd been.

'I was in school, at Port Kalamathi,' he said, his eyes shifting to the window. 'I went back to school and stayed there until I was eighteen.'

'Boarding school?'

He nodded.

'And then what?' She wished she didn't feel this curiosity, but how could she not wish to understand?

'I joined the military.'

This didn't surprise her. From the first moment she'd seen him, she'd felt he was some kind of real-life warrior. A Trojan, brought back to life.

'And did you enjoy it?'

He paused, apparently analysing that question before answering. 'Yes.'

'Why?'

His smile was tight. 'Tolmirós is a peaceful country. We do not fight wars. Our military training is the best in the world, yet we rarely have cause to require our soldiers.' He shrugged. 'I learned discipline and self-reliance.'

'I can't help thinking these are qualities you already had in spades.'

He shrugged. 'Perhaps.'

There was silence, except for the whirr of the engines as the pilot brought the plane lower and lower, over the dozens of small islands, including the one they were to land on.

'How do you get from one island to the next?' she asked.

'We have a huge ferry network. Look.' He pointed and now she saw dozens of boats moving in the water. 'See the way the islands seem to shimmer?' he asked rhetorically. 'Tolmirós is referred to as the Diamond Kingdom. Each island is like a gem in the midst of the sea.'

She nodded, the magic of that description settling

against her chest. The plane dropped lower and lower and it almost felt as though it might land in the ocean. But then land emerged from the depths of the sea and, beyond it, a runway, pale grey, lined with bright red flowers. The plane touched down with a soft thud and instinctively she looked to Leo. He lay where he was, fast asleep, and her heart gave a little tug.

Matthias was watching her; she could feel his gaze and it dragged on her like a tangible force. Slowly, of their own volition, her eyes raised to his.

Her breath locked in her throat; her body was frozen. Her very soul was arrested by the sight of this man she'd lost her head to three years earlier, a man who was so much more than that. He was a king, a ruler of a country, and all that implied.

Hadn't she detected that latent power in him, even when they'd been together back then? Hadn't she known he was someone to whom command came easily?

There was an intensity in his expression, a look of hungry determination, and her pulse raced hard and fast, her heart struggling to keep up with her blood's demands. When he spoke, it was with a contained sense of strength.

'Did you really attempt to find me?'

The question was so quiet she almost didn't hear it, like catching a swirling ribbon on a hazy night.

'It was impossible,' she murmured.

'I intended it to be so.'

The words were sharp in her sides. 'You had an easier job of forgetting me than I did you,' she said simply.

He looked as though he was about to say something, his expression taut, but then he turned away from her, his eyes roaming towards Leo.

The little boy was waking now, twisting his chubby, robust body against the flat chair, starfishing his legs out so that Frankie smiled unknowingly.

'Mama?' The plane was still moving forward but they'd landed, and Frankie unbuckled her belt and stood, crossing the aisle and undoing his seat belt. He wriggled into a sitting position, from which she plucked him onto her hip. 'Where we?'

'In an aeroplane. Do you remember?' He'd been half asleep when they'd boarded the flight. He still wore his little emoji-themed pyjamas, a gift from her parents at Christmas.

'No.' He shook his head and she smiled softly. 'Who's that?' Leo pointed a finger at Matthias.

'A friend of Mummy's,' she said quickly, earning a swift look of rebuke from Matthias.

'I'm your father, Leo,' he said over the top of her, and now it was Frankie's turn to volley back an expression of outright rage. Her lips compressed and her eyes held a warning.

'Father?' Leo blinked from Frankie to Matthias.

'Your daddy.' The words were said softly but when Matthias looked at Frankie she felt a sharp dagger of judgement. Of anger. She held his gaze, determined to show him she wasn't going to back down from this fight—or any.

'Daddy?' Leo's eyes went huge. 'You say Daddy so kind!' Leo enthused, and Frankie's heart clenched in her chest. She had told Leo that, and many other things. She'd invented a father for Leo that he could be proud of, needing her son to believe a wonderful man had been a part of his creation, even when he couldn't be a part of his life.

'We're going to stay with Daddy for a while,' Frankie said gently, ignoring the way Matthias's eyes were resting on her with startling intensity. 'Would you like that?'

Leo's lower lip stuck out and he shook his head stubbornly. Frankie dipped her head forward and hid a smile in her son's curls. Let King Matthias, who 'always got what he wanted' suck on that!

'Are you sure?' he asked teasingly, as though he wasn't remotely bothered by Leo's rejection. 'Because I happen to have a swimming pool right outside my bedroom,' he said. 'And you may use it any time.'

'A pool?' Leo tilted his head to one side in a gesture that was so reminiscent of Matthias that Frankie's chest throbbed. 'What a "pool"?'

'What's a pool?' Matthias's gaze lifted to Frankie's, subtle accusation in his eyes. 'How can you not know this? It's like the biggest bath tub you can imagine,' he said, not looking away from Frankie. 'The water is warm and salty, and you can kick and splash to your heart's content.'

'Mummy says no splashing in the bath!' Leo was dubious.

Matthias's eyes held Frankie's for a moment longer and she fought an instinct to defend herself, to defend her parenting, before dropping her gaze to Leo's. She breathed out, not having realised she'd been holding her breath until then. 'In a pool you may splash.'

Leo jumped up and down on Frankie's lap, his excitement at this relaxation in the usual rules apparent.

'Do you know what else?' Matthias leaned forward, smiling in a way that caused Frankie's breath to catch once more. 'We are very near the beach. You can go swimming whenever you like.'

Leo gleefully clapped his little hands together.

'What else do you like to do?'

That was it. Leo began to speak as best he was able, and Matthias listened and nodded along, even when Frankie was certain he couldn't understand half of what the toddler was offering.

The plane drew to a stop and the cabin crew opened the door—sultry heat immediately blew in, replacing the climate-controlled cool of the aircraft. There was sunshine on the breeze and Frankie sucked it in, deep inside her lungs, pressing her head back against the seat for a moment, letting the air stir through her body, praying it would bring a sense of calm and acceptance to her.

She had no choice but to marry him. She could even see the sense of what he'd suggested. He wasn't just a mere man—a mortal amongst mortals. He was a king, and she'd been foolish enough to sleep with a stranger—she hadn't cared who he was; she hadn't wanted or needed to know anything about him, besides the fact that she'd wanted him with an intensity that had refused to be quelled. And so they'd found themselves in bed—he'd been so experienced and charming that what little instinct she might have had to pause, to wait, had completely evaporated.

She let out a small sigh of impatience. Why bother analysing the past? It had happened, and she couldn't even say with any honesty that she wished it hadn't. Sleeping with Matthias had given her Leo, and not for all the gold in the world would she wish him away.

Nor, if she were completely honest, would she wish she hadn't slept with Matthias. He hadn't deserved her, he sure as heck hadn't deserved her innocence, but he remained, to this day, one of the best experiences of her life.

An experience she wanted to repeat?

For a second she allowed herself to imagine that future, to imagine Matthias making love to her, the nights long with passion, rent with the noise of her pleasure and delirious need, her insides slicked with moist heat.

Foreign voices filled the plane and she looked up to find Matthias watching her, even as Leo chattered to him. Heat burned her cheeks, the direction of her thoughts warming her, and she was sure he knew, and understood; she was sure he was watching her with the same sense of heated arousal.

Frankie forced herself to look past him, to the cabin crew who were making their way into the plane. A woman was at the front and she held a garment bag in her hands. No, several, Frankie noted with disinterest.

Matthias stood and spoke to his servants in his native tongue. Their deference was fascinating to observe. All bowed low and, though they spoke in their own language, she could hear the awe with which they held him.

'This is Marina.' Matthias turned to Frankie, his expression unreadable. 'She's going to help you get ready.'

'Ready for what?'

'Arriving at the palace.'

'But… I am ready.'

He looked at her long and hard, his dark gaze moving from her hair to her face and then to her clothes and, though she was wearing one of her favourite dresses, the way he looked at her made her feel as though she were dressed in a potato sack.

'What?' she asked defiantly, tilting her chin and glaring at him as though his scrutiny hadn't affected her in the slightest degree.

'You are my fiancée,' he reminded her. 'The future Queen of Tolmirós. You will feel more comfortable dressed for that role.'

She bit down on her lip and if they'd been alone she might have had a few choice phrases to utter. Instead, she stood up, keeping Leo pinned to her hip.

'I'm sorry if I don't meet your high standards, Your Majesty,' she said jerkily, panic rising inside her at the enormity of what she was going to do.

'My standards are beside the point,' he said quietly, with all the reasonableness she had failed to muster. 'This is about what will be expected of you. And Leo.' As though their child was an afterthought, he gestured to an old woman in the huddle of staff.

Her smile was kind, her face lined in a way Frankie

found instantly appealing. She looked like a woman who laughed a lot.

'This is Liana,' Matthias said, his expression unchanging as he nodded at the older woman. Emotion stirred in Liana's green eyes though, feelings Frankie couldn't begin to comprehend. The older woman's smile dropped—just for a fraction of a second. Then her attention homed in on Leo and it was as though a firework had been set off beneath her.

'Liana was my nanny, as a boy,' Matthias explained, watching as Liana moved between them and began making clacking noises at Leo. He grinned in response and then clapped his hands together. Liana did likewise and laughed, rocking back on her heels so her slender frame arched.

'May I?' she asked, a cackled question, presumably directed at Frankie, though Liana didn't take her eyes off Leo.

'I...' Frankie didn't want to hand Leo over, though. On some instinctive level, she ached to hold him close, to keep him near her.

She stared at Matthias and perhaps a hint of her panic showed itself in her eyes because his expression tightened and a pulse jerked at the base of his jaw. 'Liana will help Leo change into more suitable clothes,' Matthias reassured her, everything about him kind, as if he were trying to calm a horse on the brink of bolting. 'While you are doing likewise.'

It was a simple suggestion, and one that made sense, but the more he made sense, the more Frankie wanted to rebel.

'I really don't see the point in changing,' she said. 'You told me there wouldn't be any photographers...'

'True—' he shrugged '—but there will be staff. Hundreds of them, all looking to see the woman who will become their Queen. Would you not feel happier wearing clothes made for a princess?'

'I'm fine,' she said curtly, dismissively. Then, for Liana's benefit, 'I'd rather stay with Leo.'

He looked as if he wanted to argue with her, as if he wanted to insist. His eyes locked onto hers, he watched her thoughtfully and then he shrugged. 'It is your decision, of course.'

As soon as they arrived at the palace, she wished she hadn't been so stubborn and short-sighted. She was wearing a nice enough dress—but it was nothing compared to the grandeur of this place.

From the outside, it looked ancient. A huge, imposing castle, with the city on one side and the ocean on the other. It formed a square, and his limousine had driven under a large archway and into a central courtyard. The walls ran on all sides and when the car stopped there was a vibrant blue carpet rolled out, leading to glass double doors that had been thrown open. Servants stood on either side. The men were in suits and the women wore dresses. Most also wore white gloves to their elbows. Many had white aprons around their waists.

All looked somehow more formally attired than Frankie. Even little Leo was a resplendent king-in-waiting. A pair of grey shorts had been teamed with knee-high blue socks, shiny black shoes and a crisp white shirt with short sleeves and round buttons that glowed like pearls. His unruly hair had been combed and tamed, parted on one side, and was sitting neatly on his head with the exception of one disobedient curl that flopped into the middle of his forehead.

The three of them sat in the back of the car—a family, yet not. Matthias regarded her carefully. When he'd held his body above hers and entered her and, upon discovering for himself that she was a virgin, he'd looked into her eyes and murmured words in his language that had taken away any pain and replaced it instead with pleasure and need, so that she'd called his name over and over, an incantation, as surely as if she were a witch.

He looked at her with the desire that had rushed his bloodstream anew two nights earlier—desire that had made him want to shelve any conversation of marriage, bloodlines and their future and simply give in to his hunger for this woman. An insatiable hunger, he suspected, even when he had every intention of spending quite some time trying to satiate it.

'Well, Frankie.' He rolled her name around his mouth, tasting it, imagining kissing it against her throat, the sensitive flesh of her décolletage, down to breasts that he longed to lavish with attention. He was hard for her, ready for her already, hungry for her always. He cleared his throat, focusing on her face, forcing himself to be patient. 'Are you ready?'

Her smile lacked warmth. 'If I say "no", will it make a difference?'

His lips twisted in a grimace of sorts and he understood then what he'd failed to see on the plane. She was nervous. She was fighting with him because she was about to step off a cliff, and she had no idea what would catch her. He leaned forward so that his face was close to hers and saw the way her breath hitched in her throat, saw the way she looked at him with a quick flash of desire that she fought to cover with a tightening of her features.

'We have to do this,' he said, wishing in that moment that it wasn't the case. That Frankie didn't have to endure a marriage she clearly hated the idea of. Wishing she was free to live her life. Wishing she was free to marry a man who loved her, just as she'd insisted marriage should be.

'Then why ask the question?' Her words were snapped out but he understood now, and he frowned, wanting to relieve her tension and knowing only one way to do so.

Leo looked from one to the other and Frankie dredged up a smile for his benefit but it was weak, watery.

'Okay?' Leo asked, his little hand curving on top of Frankie's. Matthias watched the gesture with a heart that was strangely heavy.

'Fine,' she said, her smile for their child's benefit.

The door was pulled open and Matthias sat for another beat of time, looking at the woman who would be his wife, and his child. She was nervous, but there was nothing for it. They had to do this. 'Let's go then.'

Three simple words but oh, how much they meant! Because it wasn't as simple as stepping out of a car—this was like crossing an invisible border, one which she could never cross back. When she stepped out of the car, she'd cease to be a private individual. She would no longer be an up-and-coming artist on the New York scene. She'd be a royal fiancée, Matthias's bride, the up-and-coming Queen, the mother of the royal heir. She would belong to this life, to Matthias, and so would Leo.

There was nothing for it though. He'd described himself as a realist, and Frankie had a degree of realism deep in her as well. Or perhaps it was better described as fatalism, she thought, watching as Matthias stepped from the car. His staff stood still, none looking at him. He reached into the car, his arms extended, and she understood what he wanted.

Leo.

Her mouth was dry, her throat parched, her pulse racing. There was no sense in refusing him—it would be easier for her to step out of the car if she weren't holding a heavy toddler in her arms. Besides, with Matthias holding their baby, no one would be looking at her, would they?

'Go with Matthias—Daddy,' she said stiffly, kissing Leo's curls before passing him towards the door. Matthias's hands curved around Leo's midsection and then Frankie shuffled closer. Curious glances slid sideways. The servants were, perhaps, not supposed to look, and yet how could they resist?

This was their future King, arriving home as a two-year-old boy. Curiosity was only natural.

'Mama?'

'I'm coming. I'm right behind you,' she promised. And she was—she had to be. There was no way on earth Matthias would ever let Leo go. She could see that as clearly as she could the brilliant blue of the sky over-head. If she wanted to be a part of her son's life, she had to accept Matthias as a part of hers.

With nerves that were jangling in her body, school-ing her features into a mask of what she hoped would pass as calm, she stepped from the vehicle.

Eyes that had been resolutely focused ahead all turned now, and it was like being in the glare of a thou-sand spotlights. Everyone looked at her, everyone saw her, and she knew what they must be thinking.

Why her?

With a sinking heart and regret that she'd refused to allow herself to be restyled as some sort of queen-in-waiting, she brazened it out. Shoulders squared, smile on her face, as though this was a happy day for her. As though she wasn't absolutely terrified.

His arm around her waist caught her off guard and for a second—a brief second—her smile dropped. Her gaze flew to his face and she saw a warning there. A warn-ing, and a look of triumph. 'Welcome home, *deliciae.*'

Home.

She had only a second to process the word. A sec-ond to wonder what the lovely-sounding *deliciae* might mean. And then his head dropped and his lips pressed to hers, and she was dropping out of that present moment and crashing into the past, when she had—briefly—lived for this exact feeling. When his kisses alone had been her reason for breathing.

It was too much—her nerves were already stretched to breaking point and his kiss was a torture and a relief, an agony and an ecstasy.

Her body, of its own accord, swayed towards him as though drunk, demanding more contact, more closeness, more everything. It was a brief kiss—chaste in comparison to how they had kissed in the past, and yet it was enough. *More* than enough to rekindle everything. Flames that she had hoped extinguished flared to life and she had no idea how to put them out again this time.

Damn him all to heck.

He lifted his head, his eyes mocking when they met hers. Embarrassment warmed her cheeks.

'Why did you do that?' she demanded, lifting shaking fingertips to her lips, feeling the strength of his passion even now, seconds after he'd ended it.

His laugh was soft and sent electric shocks down her spine.

'Because you were nervous,' he said quietly. 'And I could think of only one way to calm you down.'

Her stomach swooped with his insightfulness, but the ease with which he could turn her blood to lava spiked her pride. With a hint of insurgency, she murmured quietly, so only he could hear, 'And what if I don't want you to kiss me?'

He laughed softly.

'Why is that funny?'

'You shouldn't issue challenges you don't wish to lose.'

'What does that even mean?'

'It means—' he leaned forward once more, his intent obvious, and yet she still didn't step back, even when she had ample opportunity to put some space between them '—I'm going to enjoy making you eat those words.' And he crushed his mouth to hers once again, his kiss a possession and a promise. A promise she knew she should fight and somehow, frustratingly, wasn't sure she wanted to...

CHAPTER FIVE

'AND THIS IS the private residence, madam.' A middle-aged man dipped his head deferentially, allowing Frankie to walk past. Her mind was already spinning, and she'd only been in the palace an hour. Exhaustion had begun to sink into her skin, making thought and attention almost impossible. Where Leo had slept on the plane, she hadn't—not a jot—and she couldn't even do the maths in that moment to work out what time it was in New York.

Late, though. Or early in the morning. No wonder she felt so wrecked.

The Private Residence was, in fact, more like a penthouse apartment. Where the rest of the palace was steeped in a sense of ancient tradition, with historic balustrades, paintings, old tapestries and glorious wallpaper giving it a sense of living history, this apartment felt completely modern.

'It was redecorated at the turn of the century,' the servant said. 'All of the wiring was renewed in this suite.' He moved deeper into the apartment. 'Would you like a tour, madam?'

'Oh, no, thank you.' What Frankie wanted more than anything was a strong coffee and to be left alone. To soften her refusal, she smiled. 'I'll find my way around just fine, I'm sure.'

'Certainly. There has not been time to properly complete Master Leo's rooms, but a start has been made,' the servant offered, gesturing down the hallway. Frankie moved in that direction as if being pulled by magic, her trained artist's eye making note of small details as she went. Here the walls were crisp white, but not perfect white—there was a warmth to them, almost as though they'd been mixed with gold or pearl. Flower arrangements were modern and fragrant, pictures were simple black and white, portraits and photographs. Artistic and interesting.

Undoubtedly the work of some palace designer or other, she thought with a twist of her lips.

'The blue door, madam,' the servant offered.

With a frown, Frankie curved her fingers around the brass door knob and turned it, pushing the door inwards. The room opened up before her and her heart sank.

How could she have contemplated turning Matthias down for even a moment? This room was every little boy's fantasy, she thought, stepping inside and turning a full circle. Leo followed behind her and he was as struck dumb at the scene as she was.

'Mine?'

Frankie couldn't form a response. She looked at him then back to the room, doubt and certainty warring inside her. 'Yes,' she acknowledged finally, moving to the small bed. Like something out of a movie, it was a pale cream, glossy, with sumptuous blue bedding, big European pillows—almost the size of Leo—and toy-soldier cushions, as if brought to life from *The Nutcracker*. A bay window overlooked a beautiful garden—'The chef's *potager*,' the servant advised with more than a touch of pride in his tone.

Though the room was filled with toys and books, they were all good quality: wooden, old-fashioned, simple. Frankie surveyed them, begrudgingly approving of their selection, their appropriateness for Leo's age and stage indisputable.

'Mine?' he asked again, lifting a set of blocks off the shelf.

'Yes,' she agreed once more.

'There you are.'

The heavily accented voice had Frankie turning and when she saw Liana smiling as she approached, it was natural for Frankie to return the gesture. She liked this woman, though she knew so little about her. There was a warmth and openness that Frankie needed—an ally in the midst of all that was new and frightening. Not to mention the fact she'd kicked off her shoes at some stage and now wore bright pink socks beneath sensible trousers—high recommendation indeed.

''Ello, Frankie.' Liana nodded, and Frankie liked her even more for using her name rather than any silly title or 'madam'. 'You like his room?'

'Oh, yes, it's perfect,' she said. 'I don't know how but someone's managed to fill it with all of the things Leo would have chosen himself, if given half a chance.'

'Ah, it is not so long since Matthias and Spiro were

boys. I remember.' She tapped a knobbly finger to the side of her head and nodded sagely.

Frankie's curiosity was stirred to life. 'Spiro?'

Liana's eyes narrowed but she didn't answer. 'You go, you go,' she said. 'I get to know.' She pointed to Leo and when he looked at her she clapped her hands together and held them out to him.

To Frankie's surprise, rather than ignoring Liana and staying with the shelves of new toys and distractions, Leo pushed to his sturdy little legs and padded over to Liana. He smiled up at the older woman, dimples dug deep in both cheeks.

'He likes you,' Frankie said, the words punctuated with the heaviness of her heart.

'And I like him.' She grinned. 'We are going to be great friends, little master Leo. No?'

'Yeah.' He nodded enthusiastically.

Liana turned back to Frankie. 'You go, relax. I keep him happy.'

Frankie was torn between a desire never to let Leo out of her sight again and a need to be alone, to have a bath, to get to grips with all that had happened. In the end, it was seeing Liana and Leo playing happily together, walking around the room and exploring it, holding hands, that made Frankie's decision for her. She turned to leave, but at the door spun back.

'Liana?' The nanny looked up, her face patient. 'Thank you. For this.' She nodded towards Leo. 'And for this,' and she gestured around the room.

'It is my pleasure,' Liana promised after a beat of silence had passed. 'It is good to have a child in the palace again, *vasillisa*.'

The servant who'd brought her to the apartment had left, so Frankie was free to explore on her own. She did so quickly, perfunctorily, looking upon the rooms as she might appraise a new subject she was painting. It helped her not to focus on the disparity in her own private situation and this degree of wealth and privilege if she saw it as an outsider rather than as one who'd been suddenly and unceremoniously sucked into these lofty ranks.

There was the small anteroom, into which they'd entered. The corridor that came this way branched off into Leo's bedroom, and another room beside it, with sofas, a small dining table and glass doors that led to a small balcony. A children's sitting room, she surmised, the décor clearly childlike yet lovely.

Another door showed a lovely bathroom—white tiles, deep tub, a separate shower and two toilets: one regular size and one lower to the ground. The last door revealed a separate bedroom and at first she thought it would be just perfect for her—and to hell with whatever form Matthias thought their marriage would take! But a longer look showed Liana's shoes tucked neatly under the bed and her jacket hung on a hook near the door.

So this was to be the nanny's accommodation?

At least that meant they wouldn't be alone in this residence! Feeling ridiculously smug, given Matthias had no doubt approved the arrangements himself, Frankie moved down the corridor and into another sitting room, this one incredibly grand. Burgundy and gold damask sofas and armchairs formed a set for six, with a marble coffee table between them, and the dining table could easily accommodate ten. It was walnut, polished, imposing, and dark. There was a bar in the corner, beside heavy oak bookshelves, and glass doors led to yet another balcony.

She moved through the room quickly, feeling out of place, like an interloper. It was impossible to imagine she'd ever feel 'at home' here.

The next room offered some improvement. A study, with modern computers, paperback books and an armchair that at least looked as if it had been made this century.

The following room was another improvement! A kitchen and an adjoining sitting room, this was far more homely, despite the large glass doors that showed an exquisite pool beyond. She imagined Matthias swimming in it, his body on display as he powerfully pulled through the water, and her throat was dry.

She swallowed, trying to push away the image, and moved into the kitchen. She almost cheered when she saw a familiar coffee machine. She searched drawers and doors until she located coffee grinds, loaded them into the basket and pressed the button. The aroma filled the room at once and she stood very still, allowing the fragrance to permeate her soul, to reassure her and relax her as only coffee could.

The pretty cup filled, she wrapped both palms around it and continued her tour. Early afternoon sunlight filtered in through the windows as she moved to the next room, and the light was so dazzling, so perfectly a mix of milk and Naples Yellow, translucent and fragile. She stood in the light for a moment, her eyes sweeping shut, before a jolt of recognition had her opening them anew.

The bed was enormous, and it sat right in the middle of the far wall. Where the wall itself was white, the bedlinen was steel-grey, with fluffy pillows and bedside tables that were devoid of anything personal. No photographs, no books, not even a newspaper.

Her heart in her throat, she moved around the bed, giving it a wide berth, heading for another door. Hoping it might lead to a bedroom, she pushed the door inwards and saw only a bathroom—this one more palatial than Leo's, with an enormous spa pressed against windows that seemed to overlook a fruit grove. No doubt if her friendly servant was nearby, he'd be able to tell her what fruit was growing there—she couldn't see from a distance.

The shower was one of those large walk-in scenarios, with two shower heads overhead and several on the walls. The controls looked like something out of a spaceship.

She backed out of the bathroom as though she'd been stung, slamming her shoulder on the way and wincing from the pain. The last remaining door showed a wardrobe—as big as her bedroom back in Queens, but only half-filled. Suits, dozens of them, all undoubtedly hand-stitched to measure, hung neatly, arranged one by one. Then shirts, crisply ironed, many still with tags attached. There were casual clothes too, and they made her stomach clench because she could imagine Matthias as he'd been *then*. Before. In New York, when he'd been simply Matt.

She sighed, propping her hips against the piece of furniture in the middle of the room. What even was it? Square-shaped, with drawer upon drawer. She pressed one out of curiosity and it sprung open. Watches! At least ten, and all very expensive-looking. She shook her head in disbelief and pushed it closed once more.

The hint of a smile danced on her lips as she imagined for a moment the ludicrousness of her clothing in this imposing space, the look of her costume jewellery next to his couture, and a laugh at that absurdity bubbled from deep inside. And if she'd been about to wonder how the heck she was even going to get her clothes, the answer presented itself in the form of a rather stylish-looking woman who introduced herself as Mathilde.

'I take your measurements,' she said, her accent French. 'And organise your wardrobe.'

'My wardrobe?'

'You will need things very quickly, but this is not your worry. I know people.'

Frankie thought longingly of the coffee she'd placed down in the immaculate bedroom next door, and the quiet time she'd been fantasising about disappeared. For, not long after Mathilde's arrival, came Angelique and Sienna, hairdresser and beautician, who set up a beauty salon in the palatial bathroom. One worked on taming Frankie's 'mom' hair, removing all traces of playdough and neglect while still managing to keep the length and natural blonde colour in place. The other waxed Frankie's brows and did her nails—fingers and toes—both tasks Frankie had neglected for far too long.

'I'm an artist,' she found herself explaining apologetically as Sienna tried her hardest to buff a splash of oil paint from Frankie's big toe nail. 'And I like to paint barefoot,' she added for good measure.

Sienna's smile was dubious and Frankie understood. How could she ever live up to this country's expectations of its Queen?

It took hours but when Frankie was at last alone once more she had to admit that the three women had worked some kind of miracle. She stared at herself in the reflection, unable to believe how…regal…she looked. Still dressed in the same clothes as New York, it no longer mattered. Her hair sat like a blonde cloud around her shoulders and she glistened all over.

Exhaustion was a tidal wave coming towards her. She showered in an attempt to stave it off and was just in the process of pulling the same dress back in place when there was a knock at the bathroom door. With a little gasp, she grabbed the dress and simply held it across her front.

'Don't come in!' she cautioned, her heart already racing into overdrive at the very idea that Matthias might stride in and pull her naked, shower-wet body into his arms.

'Of course not, madam.' Mathilde's soft accent came through with a hint of indignation. 'Only I tell you there are some things in your wardrobe now. Not a lot, but enough to start.'

'Oh.' Disappointment fired inside her; how she resented it! 'Thank you.'

'You're welcome, madam.'

Frankie reached for one of the sumptuous robes and wrapped it around herself, luxuriating for a moment in its glamorous softness before moving out of the bathroom. This side of the apartment was empty but still she moved quickly, lest another interruption came to pass and she gave into temptation, pressing her body to Matthias's and begging him to… She pushed the thought out of her mind determinedly, slipping into the wardrobe.

One side was filled with his clothes. She cast a guilty look towards the door before moving to his clothes and running her hand over them, feeling their fabric, imagining them on his body, remembering the warmth and strength of his physique. A deep need opened up inside her gut—she feared there was only one solution.

When she emerged a few moments later, Matthias was in the kitchen, the living invocation of her fantasies. Awareness jerked inside her, desire heavy, the pulse between her legs running riot at the sight of him like this. It was strange, but it was the first moment it truly hit Frankie that this was *their* home. That they would live here, side by side. For how long?

Her pulse ratcheted up a notch.

'You've toured the residence?' he prompted, lifting his head and pinning her with those intelligent grey eyes of his.

'Yeah.' It was croaky and faint; she cleared her throat. 'Yes.' Balling up her courage, she walked towards him, pleased with herself for at least remembering how to walk calmly. 'There only seems to be one bedroom spare,' she murmured.

He looked at her, a smile playing about his lips. 'Was that a question?'

Damn him! 'You can't expect me to…'

'Share your husband's bedroom?'

She fidgeted with her fingers, and then stopped when she realised what a betraying gesture it was. 'Yes.' She forced her eyes to hold his.

'Are we back to pretending you don't feel the same desire I do?'

She opened her mouth and closed it again. How could she deny her desire, after the kiss they'd shared earlier? Surely he'd tasted her response, felt her need.

'No,' she said softly, her eyes locked onto his with a defiance that gave her some kind of courage. 'But feeling something and acting on it are two different concepts.'

His eyes flared, perhaps showing his surprise at her admission. 'So they are.' He leaned a little closer and her stomach swirled. 'You do not need to worry, Frankie. When we sleep together it will be because you beg me to make love to you, not because I cannot control myself while we happen to be sharing a mattress. *Bene?*'

'I…'

'It is just a bed,' he said, making her feel naïve and childish. 'And I am away often.'

'I…'

He lifted a finger, placing it softly against her lips. 'If you do not adjust to me in your life, then I will have a new room made for you,' he said, and though the offer should have pleased her, it didn't. If she'd felt childish before, she felt babyish now—and like a complainer too. 'Just try it my way.'

It was so reasonable. So measured. 'I just presumed we'd have separate rooms,' she explained, forcing a smile to her lips.

He nodded once, his eyes latched to hers. 'Gossip spreads like wildfire. I don't need servants talking about our marriage before there's even been a marriage. Nor do I want it splashed over the tabloids that my convenient wife and heir are all for show.'

'But we are,' she said with a tilt of her head, relieved to say the words, to remind herself as much as anything.

'He is my heir,' Matthias murmured. 'And you will be my wife. There is nothing dishonest in that.'

She bit back whatever she'd been about to say, nodding instead. He was right. She'd agreed to this, and she'd known what his terms were. There was no sense demeaning herself by arguing over such a trivial point.

'You'll meet your valet tomorrow,' he said, changing the subject. 'She'll help you with anything you require.'

'Valet?'

'Your point-of-contact servant. The head of your house.'

'I… I don't need that.'

He sent her a look of sardonic amusement. 'You will receive over a thousand invitations every year to social events. Then there's the dozens and dozens of requests for you to serve as a spokesperson for charities, to fundraise on their behalf and raise their profile. Each of these will require a response, and it will be impossible for you—on your own—to know which are worthy of your consideration and which are not.'

Frankie was struck dumb momentarily. 'But why would so many people want…? I mean…'

'You will be Queen—and people will presume you have the ear of the King. There is power in your position, and it is natural that many will want to use that to their advantage.'

'But I won't have the ear of the King,' she said, shaking her head and walking towards the enormous windows that looked over the mysterious fruit grove.

'Nobody will be aware of that. To the outside, our marriage will appear to be a love match—it's natural people will presume I listen to your counsel.'

Bitterness twisted inside her, and loss too—a deep and profound sense of grief at the picture he'd so easily painted. The kind of marriage she'd always dreamed she might one day be a part of. The true sense of belonging she'd sought all her life. The thoughts were dark, depressing. She stamped them out, focusing on the business at hand. 'And my valet will manage all that for me?'

'Your secretary will.'

She frowned, not taking her eyes off the trees below. 'We were talking about a valet.'

'I said the valet is the head of your house. There will be around ten members of staff—not including your security detail—who report to your valet.'

At that she turned to face him, but wished she hadn't. The sight of him, one hip propped against the kitchen counter, watching her thoughtfully, jolted her heart painfully, as though she'd been shocked with electricity. 'Matt—' she used the diminutive form of his name without thinking '—I don't want this.'

His eyes narrowed thoughtfully. 'Why not?'

'It's just strange. I can't see that I'll need that many people working for me.'

'You wish to fire someone then?'

She opened her mouth to say something and then slammed it shut; he had her jammed into a tight corner there and undoubtedly knew it. She shook her head. 'No, I just…'

'Relax, Frankie. You will adapt to all this, I promise.'

'That's easy for you to say. You grew up with this; it's normal for you.'

He shrugged. 'And it will become normal for you.' He stood up straighter and walked towards her, opening the large glass doors. Warmth billowed in from the sunny afternoon beyond. He gestured for her to precede him onto the balcony and, curious, she did. The terracotta tiles were warm beneath her feet. Out here, the fruit trees had a delightful fragrance. She breathed in deeply, letting the smell roll all the way down to her toes.

She was in a foreign country with a man she hadn't seen in years, a man she'd slept with and then lost all contact with, a man who had fathered her son, and yet, ridiculously, standing beneath that milky sun with the citrusy fragrance like a cloud around her, the colours all green and blue with splashes of bold red where geraniums were growing, she felt completely and utterly at ease.

'My valet will coordinate with yours with regard to the wedding plans. The date has been set for two weeks' time.'

The sense of relaxation evaporated. 'Two weeks?' She jerked her head towards his. He was watching her, those eyes imprinted on her brain like ghosts.

He appeared to misunderstand her. 'This is the soonest it can be. No sooner,' he explained. 'It is necessary to give people time to travel—foreign dignitaries, royals, diplomats.'

'But...what's the rush?'

His lips were a tight line in his face. 'I have a two-year-old who, at this moment, is illegitimate and has no claim on my throne. If I were to die tomorrow, the country would not have an heir. Yet here he is, a living, breathing child of mine—you cannot see that there is a rush to marry and legally make him mine?'

Frankie bit down on her lower lip, nodding even as she tried to make sense of that. 'But you're his father—there's no doubt of that. Surely you could adopt him or—'

'Adopt *my own son*?' There was a look of cold rejection on his face, as though adopting Leo would be the worst thing in the world.

Frankie's stomach swooped and for a moment the wounds of her childhood were flayed open. 'I only meant there must be another way to legally empower him as your heir,' she said, so softly the words were almost swallowed on the breeze.

'If there was, do you think I would have been so insistent on marrying you?'

* * *

He'd gone too far. He could see it in the way all the colour had drained from her face. No, from her whole body! She was as white as the sand of Makalini Beach, her eyes green and awash with hurt.

Damn it!

But he was in shock, still trying to make sense of this, trying to see the best way forward for both of them. The last thing he wanted was to argue with Frankie. None of this was her fault, and he admired her courage and strength in taking her place beside him.

He exhaled softly, turning the words over in his heart before speaking them to her. 'I hate knowing that he was out there for two and a half years and I knew nothing of him.'

She made a strangled noise; he took it to be one of understanding.

'The laws of succession are archaic and unchangeable. Even the fact he is born out of wedlock will require a DNA test to satisfy my country's parliament. They must ratify his legitimacy and—'

'Wait—just a second,' she interrupted urgently. 'You're actually going to get our child paternity tested?'

He turned to her, confused now by the anger that had surged into her face. Relieved too, as it made her cheeks glow pink once more. 'It is necessary,' he said.

'No way.'

Her refusal intrigued him and alarmed him in equal measure. 'Why not?' He bit the words out from teeth that were suddenly clenched tight. Was it possible she'd lied about Leo's paternity?

But why would she?

'Because he's your son! He can't be anyone else's, unless it was an immaculate conception,' she said with quiet insistence. 'And because I don't want him to think he had to have a blood test to prove to his own father what's blatantly obvious when you look at the two of you together.'

He relaxed once more—because, of course, she was right. Leo was a carbon copy of not only himself, but of Spiro too. As quickly as his brain absorbed that fact, it moved onto another she'd revealed. 'You're saying you haven't slept with anyone since me?'

'I...' She swept her eyes shut and shook her head. When she looked at him again a moment later she was calm—cool and somehow dismissive. She was excellent at doing that—at submerging whatever she was feeling beneath a mask of unconcern. He'd seen her do it numerous times and on each occasion he felt overwhelmed by a desire to work out exactly how he could shake that mask loose. He knew one way, of course. One very tempting, very distracting way...

'I'm saying you're the only person who could be his father.'

'Is that not the same thing?'

'No.'

His gut clenched and a dark sensation speared through him. It wasn't jealousy exactly—it was... possession. Primal, ancient, animalistic possession. He didn't want to think of her sleeping with any other man—ever.

'Have there been other men?' he asked, the question

direct, and he had the satisfaction of seeing her mask slip for a second.

'Why do you care?'

'Because I like thinking I'm the only man who's known the pleasure of your body,' he said simply, unapologetically.

Heat stained her cheeks and he could resist no longer. He moved to where she stood on the balcony, bracing a hand on either side of her. 'That's kind of chauvinistic.'

His lips twisted in a smile. 'Yes.'

And then, to his surprise, she smiled, a genuine smile that made the corners of her eyes crinkle and it felt as if the sun was forcing its way into his chest. He stared at her, his own face unknowingly tense, rigid, frozen by the radiance of her expression. 'At least you admit it.'

He continued to stare, drinking in her beauty, but the smile dropped almost immediately and an air of seriousness surrounded them.

'You told him about me?'

She swallowed, her eyes half-closed, shielding herself from him. 'Yes.'

'You told him I was kind?' he prompted, remembering the remark their son had made on the flight over.

She was defensive. 'I wanted him to believe his father was a good man. I wanted him to be proud of you.'

Matthias's breathing was shallow. 'Why?'

She toyed with her fingers in front of her, weaving them together. 'One day, he'll be old enough to ask about you. I didn't want him to fill in the gaps in the meantime. I didn't want him to think…'

Her words trailed into nothingness.

'Go on,' he urged desperately.

'I didn't want him to think he wasn't wanted.' She cleared her throat. 'I told him you were good and kind and funny but that you live far away from us, but that…'

'Yes?' The word was quick to escape from him, an impatient hiss.

'That you think of us often. That you look into the stars and think about the stars above us.' There was defiance in her tone now. 'It's for him, not you.'

His chest felt heavy. She'd created a myth for their son, a myth of him as a good, kind, decent man—she'd done the opposite of what he might have imagined a woman in her shoes doing: she'd praised him and spoken of him in a way that would make their son want to know his father.

It was impossible not to look at her with growing respect, with appreciation. He wasn't sure he'd deserved any of that.

'I don't want him to have a paternity test,' she said quietly, but with a strength that called to him. 'I don't want him to think…'

'To think what, Frankie?' he pushed when her words trailed off into the air.

'To think he wasn't wanted.' She lifted her gaze to his and there was a haunted quality to her expression, a hurt he couldn't comprehend. 'I don't want him to think he had to have a blood test before you'd let him into your life.'

He expelled a breath, his nostrils flaring as he instinctively rejected her take on the situation. 'It is merely a formality.'

'It's unnecessary.' Again, he felt her tender insistence deep in his gut and a protective instinct surged inside him—though what he was wanting to protect her from, he couldn't have said.

'He's your son,' she continued quietly, lifting one hand to his chest and pressing it just above his heart.

And emotions flooded him—paternal pride, completeness, rightness—relief that it was this woman who'd borne him a son and heir. His words were thick with all his feelings when he dredged them from deep within his soul. 'And soon the whole world will know it.'

CHAPTER SIX

MATTHIAS COULDN'T REMEMBER when he'd last slept for longer than an hour or two. He was bone-weary, exhausted to the depths of his soul, but the sight of Frankie fast asleep in his bed arrested him and energised him all at once and he found his feet reluctant to move.

The way she'd smiled at him earlier that day had stayed with him all afternoon, replaying in his mind, so that he had rushed through his commitments, hoping to see her again, to see if he could make her smile once more. Not that he could say what he'd done to change her mood—it wasn't like in New York, three years earlier, when they'd both smiled often and freely.

He'd wanted to see her again, but events had conspired to keep him from dining with her—a problem at the embassy in Rome—and so now she was fast asleep.

Her long blonde hair was drawn around her shoulder like a skein of gold and her breathing was slow and rhythmic. Her lips, parted and pink, were so perfect, and he remembered instantly how they'd felt when she'd kissed him in New York, years earlier.

Tentatively at first, and then with the madness that

had overtaken them. He remembered how she'd felt in his arms downstairs earlier today, when he'd taken her by surprise and kissed her, and he remembered the moment when she'd become pliant in his arms. He could identify the exact moment when she'd lost a part of herself to this madness. He'd known he could have deepened the kiss, that he could have taunted her with their desire and turned her into a jumble of nerves and responses in his arms, but he hadn't.

He'd stemmed his own needs, respecting her boundaries, knowing deep down how overwhelmed she must be. Not just by his position as King, and her son's place in the country's order of succession, not even by her future as Queen. But by this, them, whatever they felt. He was a man of far greater experience, of greater years, and yet he still found their chemistry explosive and somehow awe-inspiring.

Even as he stood by the bed, watching her gentle exhalations, desire flooded his system and he wondered how she'd respond if he reached for her. If he strode to the bed, put a hand on her shoulder and stirred her to wakefulness, if he pressed his lips to the soft flesh at the base of her throat that had always driven her wild...

And as though his thoughts had pushed into hers, she moved in her sleep, her eyes blinking open and landing straight on him. Breath that had been slow suddenly stopped altogether as she stared at him.

It was just after midnight, and magic was thick in the air—magic with the power to bring the past into the present.

'Matt?' She blinked, frowning, pushing up so that the sheet dropped to reveal the soft swell of her cleavage. There was nothing sexy about the singlet she was wearing or at least it shouldn't have been. But somehow it was, and he was groaning with side-splitting need.

He swallowed—hard—and he was hard all over, his body wound tighter than a spring.

'I was… You were just…' In the soft milky moonlight he saw her cheeks flush pink and he took a step deeper into the room despite every bone in his body telling him it was wrong.

'Yes?' The word came out thick and gravelled. He cleared his throat, watching her intently.

'I thought I was dreaming.'

His body fired. Desires he'd already been battling surged inside him. 'Was it a good dream?' he asked, taking the rest of the steps necessary to bring him level with the bed. His own side yawned empty and cold. Duty and responsibility were on his side of the bed, but temptation lay here, and he was oh, so tempted.

'I…' She frowned and lifted a hand to the strap of her top. His eyes followed the action and at the sight of the outline of her nipples, straining hard against the fabric of her shirt, he suppressed a groan.

There was the right thing to do, and there was what they both wanted and needed.

Ignoring common sense, he caught her hand on her shoulder, holding it low, and then, his eyes locked onto hers, loaded with challenge, he oh-so-slowly traced his fingertips over her flesh, easing the strap lower, not higher. Her skin lifted with fine goosebumps and her breath stalled in her throat. Her eyes were pleading and he watched her, challenge in every line of his face.

'What did you dream?' he asked, his other hand reaching for the strap that still sat on her shoulder. He didn't push it downwards though. He simply looped his fingers beneath it, his eyes on her face, waiting, still, frozen in time, impatient to know what she was going to say.

'I dreamed… I was… It was years ago,' she said huskily, her beautiful face clouded with uncertainty.

'And do you dream of me often?'

Her slender throat moved visibly as she swallowed and her eyes swept shut, perhaps in an attempt to block him from seeing her thoughts in that expressive face of hers. 'No,' she whispered.

'Liar.' His laugh was without humour. 'I think you dream of me frequently. Perhaps every night, even.'

At her harsh intake of breath he bent lower and, knowing he should stop this madness, he crushed his lips to hers, swallowing the little moan she made, tasting her sweetness, and memories and feelings rushed back at him because she tasted, she *felt* exactly as she had done then and his whole body rejoiced at that familiarity and rightness.

Her mouth was parted and he slipped his tongue inside, duelling with hers, reminding her of this need, and she whimpered into the kiss before her hands lifted and her fingers tangled in the hair at the nape of his neck, just as she had then. Her body lifted, her breasts crushed to his chest and he swore in his own language as impatience threatened to burst him wide open.

'Tell me you dreamed of this,' he demanded, his fingers pushing the straps down now, so her breasts were free of the flimsy garment, and he cupped them greedily in his palms, feeling their weight, their generous roundness tightening his body so his arousal strained against his pants and his whole body ached for her in a way that defied sense and reason.

She had! Oh, she'd dreamed of this again and again and in the groggy half-awake state she was in it was almost impossible to believe this wasn't just a dream. But his hands on her were real—everything about this was real. She arched her back hungrily and pulled him with her hands, pulling him down on top of her, ignoring the voice in her head that was shouting at her to see reason and make this stop.

It was the witching hour and she was bewitched. He was strong, and big, and though she pulled him he came at his own pace, slowly easing his body weight on top of hers then rolling his hips so his arousal pressed to her womanhood. A sharp dagger of need perforated her senses. It was achingly, perfectly familiar. She needed him.

'Please,' she whimpered, knowing she was stranded on this wave of desire, that she was stranded on an island of sexual craving from which there was no other relief.

He rolled his hips again and his body, so hard and heavy, pressed to her feminine core, stoking her pulse, her needs, her wants. Pleasure was a cloud carrying her away, but reality was gravity, dragging her back to earth.

It had all been so easy for him that weekend three years ago. He'd looked at her and wanted her and she'd fallen into bed with him, despite having intended to save her virginity for the man she was going to marry. She'd had no defences for someone like him, no experience with men at all, really.

And now? She was falling for it again, letting desire make a mockery of all her good intentions.

Was she really going to be this woman? A woman who let passion control her actions and dictate her life. Was she really going to fall into the habit of sleeping with someone she desired even when love wasn't a part of the equation?

'We can't do this.' She shook her head, pulling away from his kiss, and now his body on hers felt like a crushing weight from which she needed to be free. She pressed her palms to his chest and felt the brief impression of his fast-racing heart before she shoved him bodily off herself and rolled out of bed.

'I can't,' she repeated, though he hadn't said a single word. He was simply watching her with the same intensity with which he'd been kissing her a moment earlier.

'I'm not going to do that.' She pulled her straps back into place, her fingers shaking so much she had to curve them into fists and hold them by her side.

He was still watching her, saying nothing, just staring, and though she was now fully dressed she felt more naked and exposed than ever before. She'd put a stop to whatever had been about to happen—but the inevitably of their coming together was still heavy in the room.

He watched her for a long time, as if seeing all the pieces of her soul. 'How come you were still a virgin, Frankie?'

The question pricked something in the region of her heart. She knew her expectations were out of step with most people's reality, but they were her feelings, her resolves. 'I…just was.'

'No.' He propped up on one elbow, apparently completely relaxed. 'I don't believe it was a matter of you having simply not slept with anyone.'

'Why not?' She challenged, her eyes sparking with his.

'Because you're a flesh and blood woman,' he murmured throatily. 'And I know for myself how sensual you are. How hungry your appetite…'

Her pulse sped up and with his eyes digging into hers she found she didn't want to lie to him. What was the point? 'I wanted to save myself for my husband.' She slid her gaze sideways, aware of how juvenile the assertion must have sounded. She focused her eyes on the wall and didn't see the look of intense concentration that overtook his features.

'Why?' A single word, rough and husky.

'I've told you: sex should mean something.' She frowned. 'I *thought* it should mean something. I was… I think sex and love should go hand in hand and when I eventually fell in love, and someone loved me, I wanted it to be something I shared with them.' When had she first started to align sex with love? She wasn't sure she'd ever know. When had she inextricably bound the two, sentiment and act, together? 'And then I met you.'

There was a self-mocking tilt to his beautiful lips. 'A man who thinks sex is for fun and love is a construct.'

Her heart stammered at the coldness of that assessment. 'A man I couldn't resist.' She shook her head, clearing the vestiges of the past from her mind. 'But that was years ago and I'm not the same person any more.' Certainty strengthened inside her. 'I guess you could say I learned my lesson.'

'We have already discussed this. I need another child, another heir…'

She ignored the cold, callous conclusion to that sentence—*in case anything happens to Leo.* 'That's an entirely separate proposition to what we were just about to do. Sleeping together because we aren't strong enough to listen to common sense, to do the right thing, is simply a matter of poor judgement.'

'You are cutting off your nose to spite your face,' he observed dryly.

His comment was utterly accurate. In putting a halt to their sensual pull she was only hurting herself because she wanted him with all of herself. She needed him. And yet she was resisting him because her pride demanded it of her. Not just her pride—her heart. Her heart, that could have so easily been his; her heart that had been hurt and ignored too many times to easily trust. 'I'm not. I'm just… I'm someone who always wanted the fairy tale,' she said quietly.

But often the most quietly voiced sentiments carried the most resonance.

'There's no such thing as fairy tales,' he said after several beats of silence had passed, and he stared at her for a long moment, his expression a mask of intensity. 'And even if there were, I could not give it to you.'

She sucked in an unsteady breath, lost for words.

'You can get back in bed, Frankie. Relax. I won't touch you unless you ask me to.' And he turned onto his side, his back to her.

Silence fell. She stood there, watching him for a moment, and when his breathing was rhythmic and steady she climbed into bed, turning her own back on him and hugging the edge of the mattress.

It was a recurrent nightmare but that didn't change the fact that it flooded Matthias with adrenalin as if it was all happening for the first time. He was back in the limousine. The smell of petrol and burning flesh filling his nostrils, his body trapped, his eyes open. His parents were dead but Spiro, beside him, was still alive.

His cries were like nothing Matthias could put into words.

'I'm coming,' he promised, pushing at the metal that was heavy on his chest. 'Just keep your eyes open.'

The driver was dead too. He couldn't see the security agent who had been travelling in the same car as them.

'I can't, Matt,' Spiro groaned, and his dark eyes were covered with tears.

'You must.' Matthias, a teenager, swore darkly into the limousine and Spiro winced. He had to get free. He had to save them.

'I'll be there in a second. Hold my hand.' He reached

out and the pain was like nothing he'd ever known before. His arm was broken. He grunted, extending it as best he was able. It was just far enough. Spiro put his smaller hand in Matthias's, and Matthias looked at them; their flesh was the same colour, their hands the same shape. But Spiro's was cold. Ice-cold, like nothing Matthias had ever known.

'Listen to me.' Matthias spoke urgently. 'I can hear sirens in the distance. Can you?' There was a bleating—from far away. 'They're coming to help you, Spiro. They're going to cut you out of this car and take you to hospital. I'll be beating you again in basketball in weeks.'

Spiro smiled—his teeth were covered in blood. Matthias's chest ached. His younger brother's eyes were heavy.

'Damn it—stay awake,' Matthias commanded, pushing at the metal once more. It budged, but only by a tiny amount. 'Damn it!' he shouted again.

'Matt…' Spiro dropped his hand and Matthias jerked his head towards his brother. Stars danced in his eyes and for a second he blacked out. When he came to the sirens were louder, and Spiro was sleeping. At least he looked like he was sleeping.

'Spiro!' Matthias pushed at the metal—it must have weighed a ton. Nothing moved. His own body was broken. Hysteria groaned inside him. 'Spiro!'

He turned towards the front of the car and wished he hadn't, when the sight of his parents' mangled bodies filled his vision. He closed his eyes and prayed, then

"4 for 4" MINI-SURVEY

We are prepared to **REWARD** you with 2 FREE books and 2 FREE gifts for completing our MINI SURVEY!

FREE Value Over **$20!**

You'll get...

TWO FREE BOOKS & TWO FREE GIFTS

just for participating in our Mini Survey!

Dear Reader,

IT'S A FACT: if you answer 4 quick questions, we'll send you 4 FREE REWARDS!

I'm not kidding you. As a leading publisher of women's fiction, we value your opinions… and your time. That's why we are prepared to **reward** you handsomely for completing our mini-survey. In fact, we have 4 Free Rewards for you, including 2 free books and 2 free gifts.

As you may have guessed, that's why our mini-survey is called **"4 for 4".** Answer 4 questions and get 4 Free Rewards. It's that simple!

Thank you for participating in our survey,

Pam Powers

To get your 4 FREE REWARDS:
Complete the survey below and return the insert today to receive 2 FREE BOOKS and 2 FREE GIFTS guaranteed!

"4 for 4" MINI-SURVEY

1 Is reading one of your favorite hobbies?
  ☐ YES ☐ NO

2 Do you prefer to read instead of watch TV?
  ☐ YES ☐ NO

3 Do you read newspapers and magazines?
  ☐ YES ☐ NO

4 Do you enjoy trying new book series with FREE BOOKS?
  ☐ YES ☐ NO

YES! I have completed the above Mini-Survey. Please send me my 4 FREE REWARDS (worth over $20 retail). I understand that I am under no obligation to buy anything, as explained on the back of this card.

☐ I prefer the regular-print edition
106/306 HDL GNVV

☐ I prefer the larger-print edition
176/376 HDL GNVV

FIRST NAME	LAST NAME

ADDRESS

APT.#	CITY

STATE/PROV.	ZIP/POSTAL CODE

READER SERVICE—Here's how it works:

▼ If offer card is missing write to: Reader Service, P.O. Box 1341, Buffalo, NY 14240-8531 or visit www.ReaderService.com ▼

BUSINESS REPLY MAIL
FIRST-CLASS MAIL   PERMIT NO. 717   BUFFALO, NY

POSTAGE WILL BE PAID BY ADDRESSEE

READER SERVICE
PO BOX 1341
BUFFALO NY 14240-8571

NO POSTAGE
NECESSARY
IF MAILED
IN THE
UNITED STATES

swore, then reached for Spiro with an arm that didn't seem to want to obey his brain's commands.

He needed to get free so he could save his brother. There was no water—the car had swerved to avoid a boulder in the middle of the road. It had flipped over into a valley and landed on its roof. But in Matthias's dream they were always on the edge of water, and slowly it seeped into the car. Not transparent like the water that surrounded his palace, but a sludgy black, then burgundy, like blood.

Spiro died and Matthias could do little more than reach for his hand.

At fifteen, he lost everyone he'd ever loved.

It would be two hours before the rescue teams could free him. Two hours in which he stared at his brother and tried not to look towards his parents. Two hours in which his heart, though still beating, ceased to feel.

'Matt?' She pushed at his shoulder; it was damp with perspiration. 'Matthias? Wake up.'

He made a noise and then sat bolt upright, so his head came close to banging hers. His eyes were wide open and when they swung to face hers they were huge and dark. The sun was not yet up but the sky had taken on a dawn tinge—gold and pink warred with silver-grey, bathing the room in a warm glow.

His breathing was rushed, but not in a good way. Not in the way hers had been the night before. He stared at her as though he was drowning and she could save him; he stared at her as though he expected her to say or do something, but she couldn't fathom what.

'Are you okay?' she asked, as slowly his face assumed its normal handsome appearance. His lips closed, his eyes shuttered, his colour returned to normal.

'I'm fine.' He swung his powerful legs off the side of the bed and cradled his head in his hands for a moment. His back was turned to her yet again, but this time she resented that.

'You had a bad dream.'

He made a guttural sound.

'Want to talk about it?'

Another grunt, then he pushed to standing and strolled towards the French windows that led to the balcony.

'I'll take that as a no,' she murmured, more to herself than him.

He heard though and turned back to face her. He was wearing boxer shorts, but it still took a monumental effort for Frankie to keep her attention trained on his face. 'It's nothing.' He pushed the window open and stepped outside. The pale curtain billowed in after him.

Not understanding why, she followed him, knowing he was seeking privacy and that she should let him have that, knowing she had no reason to go after him. Understanding he wouldn't welcome the intrusion but going anyway. She padded across the room, swallowing a yawn as she went, and emerging on the balcony.

He was staring at the ocean. She followed the direction of his gaze, unable to ignore the appreciative gasp that was a natural response to the sheer beauty before her. In the early morning light the sea shimmered silver and flashes of pre-dawn sunlight made the ripples

appear to glisten like diamonds and topaz. The sky itself was a work of art she could never replicate—colours that didn't appear in any manmade palette, and
the combination of which, if she'd pushed them into
service, would be almost garish.

'He was only nine years old.' Matthias surprised her
by speaking. She drew her attention back to his face and
something in her chest skidded to a halt. His expression was the most sombre she'd ever seen—not just on
Matthias, but on any human being.

'Who?'

He looked at her then, but as though he didn't really
see her. His expression didn't shift. 'My brother. Spiro.'

Liana had mentioned Spiro, and now it made sense.
Her heart broke for him.

'He was nine when he died.'

Grief clutched at Frankie's chest. 'How?'

'A car accident.'

'I'm so sorry.'

It was the wrong thing to say. He withdrew from her
visibly, shrinking into his hard-edged shell.

'It is what it is.'

'Don't do that,' she murmured, shaking her head. An
early morning breeze came from the ocean, carrying
with it the tang of sea salt and ruffling Frankie's hair.
She caught it with her fingertips and held it over one
shoulder. 'Don't act like it doesn't matter. You're talking
about your brother's death. It's okay to say you're upset.'

If anything, his features tightened. 'What good can
come from being upset?' he asked, the words flat, turning away from her, showing he didn't expect an answer.

'Plenty.' She gave one anyway. 'Being upset, talking about how you feel, helps you move on. Helps you process…'

He shook his head. 'Why should I get to move on when Spiro has died?' He gripped the railing and leaned over it a little, staring at the ground beneath. 'Sometimes I think that if I can just reach for him in my dream, it won't have happened. That I will wake up and he will be here. Sometimes I think the accident was the nightmare, only I don't know how to rouse myself from it.'

Frankie made a small sound of sympathy.

'There is no processing this.' His eyes were hollow when he turned to her. 'There is no moving on from it. And I don't *want* to move on. Spiro is a part of me— his life, and his death. I live for both of us.'

Her fingertips ached to touch him, to comfort him, only the memory of how incendiary contact with this man could be was still alive in her gut, fresh in her mind, and so with great determination she kept her hands at her sides.

'Your parents died in the accident as well?' she murmured gently.

His response was a curt nod but the pain in his eyes was palpable, his emotions strong and fierce.

'Oh, Matt,' she murmured, and determination gave way to sympathy and an innate need to comfort him, to ease his suffering. She lifted her fingertips to his shoulder and gently traced his flesh. He was still so warm. A kaleidoscope of butterflies launched in her belly. The sun rose higher; gold slanted across her face. 'I can't imagine what that was like for you.'

'An adjustment,' he grunted, his nostrils flaring, his eyes pinning her to the spot.

She looked at him with obvious disbelief. 'Stop acting like you're too tough to care. No one can go through something like that and not have it change them. You must have been…'

'It changed me,' he stated, interrupting her with a voice that was weighted down by his feelings. 'It changed me a great deal. At fifteen I still believed my parents were infallible, that my sovereignty was guaranteed and that Spiro would spend his life driving me crazy with annoying questions and demands for attention. At fifteen I believed that I was the future King and would one day have the power to do and fix and make just about anything. I truly thought I was omnipotent.'

She nodded slowly, unconsciously bringing her body closer to his. 'I think most teenagers feel that—royal or not.'

'Maybe so.' He didn't smile but his eyes dropped to her lips, tracing their soft roundness with visible distraction. 'By the time I turned sixteen I saw the world for what it is.'

Silence throbbed around them, emotional and weary.

'And what's that?' she prompted after a moment.

'Transient. Untrustworthy.'

She shook her head and the hand that had been tentatively stroking his shoulder curved around it now, so only her thumb swept across his warm flesh. When he still didn't look at her, she lifted the other hand to his shoulder, needing more contact, as though through her touch alone she could reassure him and somehow fix this.

'What happened to you is a terrible tragedy,' she said quietly. 'But you can't let it rob you of your own happiness. Your parents wouldn't want that. Your brother wouldn't either. You say you're living for Spiro, but how can you be when you take such a dim view of all there is out there?'

'I am a realist, remember?' he said, breathing in deep, so his chest moved forward and brushed against her front. Her nipples tingled at the unintentional contact.

'A realist? I don't know, Matt. Sometimes I think you're nudging into pessimist territory.'

His eyes held hers and the air between them was thick, like the clouds before a storm. 'Is that so bad?'

'I…' Her mind was finding it hard to keep up. She looked at him, shaking her head, but why?

'Maybe, over time, you'll change me,' he said and then his smile was cynical and the air returned to normal. She blinked, like waking up from her own dream.

'I'm not sure people really change so easily.'

He stepped out of her reach and nodded curtly. 'Nor am I.'

CHAPTER SEVEN

'JUST A LITTLE this way, please, madam,' the photographer urged, holding a slender tanned arm in the air.

Frankie followed his instructions, but the smile she had pinned to her face earlier was starting to feel as if it was held in place via glue.

'Perfect. Just a few more—over near the balcony.'

The afternoon sun was streaming in like arrows of gold, no less dazzling than it had been earlier that day, when they'd stood on a different balcony and watched the dawn crest over the ocean. But then he'd been wearing only boxer shorts and the trauma of his dream had clung to him like a dark cloak she'd needed to break him free of. Now, Matthias looked every inch the handsome King. A dark suit with a cream tie, his eyes glinted in his tanned face. Black hair had been styled back from his brow, and it was all she could do not to simply stare at him.

Mathilde had presented Frankie with a cream dress for the formal engagement announcement photo session—it was long and had a ruffle across one shoulder that fell to her waist before swishing out into a narrow skirt, all the way to her ankles. Teamed with a pair of heels, she at least had a small advantage on her usual height, so she didn't feel so small when standing beside Matthias.

'It has been forty minutes,' Matthias bit out, lifting his gold wristwatch and staring at the time. 'Surely you have enough?'

The photographer, busy looking at the digital screen on the back of the camera, glanced up and blinked, then nodded. 'Almost, Your Majesty,' he promised. 'Just five more minutes.'

Frankie risked a glance at Matthias's face; it was forbidding and oh, so regal. These engagement portraits were going to make them look as if they were on their way to a funeral rather than a wedding.

'Do you need a break, *deliciae*?' Matthias looked directly at her and her heart thumped in her chest.

She shook her head. 'I'm fine. You?'

He grimaced in response. 'Hardly my preferred way to spend time.'

'Just against the railing, please, sir. Madam.'

Matthias assumed a nonchalant, bored pose and Frankie stood beside him. The photographer shook his head. 'Lean into him a bit more. Like this—' The photographer tilted his head and smiled.

Frankie compressed her lips and looked up at Matthias before moving. He was watching her, his expression sardonic.

With a small sigh, Frankie did as the photographer had suggested, but it was like being exposed to flames. Her head rested on his pectoral muscle; she could hear his heart, feel his warmth. Her smile was barely there, a whisper on her face—how could she smile when standing upright was such an effort? Matthias's hand curved around her back and his fingers splayed wide, moving ever so slightly up and down, up and down, so heat and warmth radiated from where he touched her.

'Smile!' the photographer reminded her. Frankie tried, but all of her was tied up in that moment in simply feeling. Sensations were overriding anything else. The desire she was trying to fight with all her being surged inside her, making her nerve-endings quiver, making her want to burst from the room and drag Matthias to bed, to reclaim what she knew they could mean to one another.

Matthias dipped his head forward and said *sotto voce*, 'You are trembling like a little leaf, *mikró*.'

She looked up at him, for a moment forgetting they weren't alone. Their eyes latched and nothing—no one—existed. They were alone on the balcony, the ancient ocean rolling in the background as it had for millennia. Grey eyes held green, and she lost herself in their depths. She lost herself in the ocean of his eyes, she fell to the bottom, she drowned on the seafloor, wrapped in sand and shells, and she cared not—she forgot everything.

His head dropped slowly, as if on a time lapse, though of course it hadn't really been so slow. To Frankie, though, it was the work of minutes: long, agonising, tense moments when her lips were tingling and her eyes were holding his and she could think of nothing else but a need to sink into his kiss. It was just a brush of his lips to hers, the lightest, most frustrating contact.

He kissed her, the photographer clicked, and her body snapped to life. The moan that escaped her lips was involuntary, just a small husky sound, and then Matthias lifted his head, his eyes not leaving Frankie's passion-ravaged face. 'It is enough,' he said and his words had a cool tone.

'Yes, sir, definitely. That's plenty. Thank you, sir.'

Matthias turned to Frankie and extended a hand, and ridiculously she almost didn't take it. Fear dogged her every move. Fear of this—what she was fighting, the certainty that this passion could subsume her every good intention and intellectual certainty that Matthias was not someone she could trust with her heart, her life, her love.

How absurd. She was overthinking it!

She took his hand, purely because the photographer was there and to refuse would have seemed churlish and strange, and walked with him through the gallery they'd been posing in earlier. At the door she let go, pulling her hand back softly and rubbing her palms together.

'So the engagement will be announced when?'

'Tomorrow.'

They continued to walk down a wide beautiful corridor, lined with enormous floral arrangements. They were fragrant and stunning.

'I need to tell my parents. They're going to be... blind-sided.'

Matthias tilted a look at her. 'Why?'

Frankie pulled a face. 'Well, I'm getting married, to a man they've never even heard of. A king, no less!'

'You're marrying your son's father,' he said laconically.

'A man they don't know from Adam.'

'Who's Adam?'

She shook her head. 'It's an expression. I mean, you're just some guy who…'

'Yes?'

She flicked her gaze to him and then looked away again. Ridiculously, she felt uncomfortable addressing the truth of what had happened between them. 'Who got me pregnant and disappeared into thin air.'

She wasn't looking at him, so didn't see the way his features tightened as though he'd been slapped. She didn't see the way a muscle jerked in his jaw and his eyes focused more intently on her face. 'I presume they think the worst of me.'

She shrugged. 'Can you blame them?'

'No.' The forcefulness of his word had her looking at him once more. 'If we had a daughter and this was her fate—'

'My fate wasn't so bad,' she said with a small grimace. 'I got Leo, remember?'

Matthias didn't acknowledge her comment. 'If I had known there was even the slightest chance of you having conceived that night, things would have been very different.'

'Different how?'

'I wouldn't have missed a moment of his life,' he said, the words rich with emotion. Foolish hurt dipped

in Frankie's gut—hurt that it was Leo alone he would
have wished to see and support. Hurt that a desire to
spend more time with her didn't enter into it, when she
had pined for his touch, for his smile, for months.

'We can't change the past,' she said softly.

'Nor can we secure the future. But here, in this moment, I promise you, Frankie, this is not how I would
have wanted things to be. You shouldn't have had to do
this alone. If I could miraculously turn time backwards
and change this, I would. With all of myself, I would…'

She swallowed, looking up at him, and she could feel
the truth of his regret, his remorse, his desire to have
been a part of this from the beginning.

'I know.'

He stared at her, long and hard, and though he didn't
speak it was as though his gaze was asking a question
of her: did she really understand that? Did she really
believe that he was not the kind of man to abandon a
young, pregnant woman? Did she know how deeply ab-
horrent that was to him?

And then, as though he saw her answer, he saw her
acceptance of his innocence, he nodded. As though
a switch had been flicked, he became a man of action. A king. A ruler. A man without doubt and self-
recriminations. 'I will call your parents and explain.'

Frankie let out a laugh. 'You've never even met my
parents!'

His eyes glowed with intent. 'I am the man you're
going to marry, the man who fathered their grandson,
even if I haven't been any kind of a father to him. I owe

it to them to explain my absence, and how I intend to remedy that.'

'Hang on.' She laughed again and was surprised to find true amusement spinning through her. His eyes clung to her smile and her heart turned over, sobering her. 'You're not...this isn't...you're not a character in a Jane Austen novel. Nor am I, for that matter. I don't need you to go to my dad and ask for permission.'

His eyes narrowed imperceptibly. 'It is a mark of respect.'

'Respect *me*,' she said, 'and my wishes, and my parents will be okay.'

'I owe them an explanation...'

'You owe *me* an explanation, not them, and you've given me one. I understand. I forgive you. They're nothing to do with this.'

'It is important to me that your parents understand I had no idea you were pregnant.'

'They know that,' she said quietly. 'What do you think I said to them?'

At this, he was very still, as though it hadn't occurred to him that she might have painted a picture of him to her family at all. 'I have no idea.'

'I told them you were an amazing man, who I couldn't contact. I told them we didn't plan to see each other again, and that it wasn't your fault I couldn't find you. I told them I'd tried—they knew about the investigator—but, ultimately, they just feel sorry for you. For what you've missed. My parents are...' She swept her eyes shut for a moment, her childhood and reality hitting her hard in that moment. 'Being parents meant everything to them. The fact you were deprived of that privilege through life's circumstances is something they were saddened by. Not angry about.'

His expression showed scepticism, but she barely registered it.

She forced a smile to her face. 'Besides, they got to be grandparents to Leo, and believe me when I tell you: no child has ever been more spoiled nor adored. No baby has ever been so hugged and kissed.'

His frown deepened. 'Yet they left you living in poverty?'

'Poverty?' She rolled her eyes now and gestured down the corridor. 'My apartment might not have been a palace, but it was hardly a slum either, Matthias. Don't be such a snob.'

His laugh was involuntary—no one had called Matthias a snob in his life.

'Mum and Dad aren't wealthy,' she said softly, a warm smile touching her lips. 'They helped when they could, but my dad has needed a heap of operations for his back and that didn't come cheap.'

Matthias's brow wrinkled.

'Insurance wouldn't cover it.' She recalled the way her father had delayed the necessary procedures, insisting he could manage, when his body gradually betrayed him. 'The last thing I wanted was for them to worry about Leo and me.'

'But you have found it difficult?'

'Financially?'

He nodded.

'Yes. But that was my choice, my business. I knew

being an artist would be hard. I have had to do things I didn't particularly like, just to get by, to support Leo. It's why I need the art show to be a success. I wanted my career to be able to support us, but in reality, who knows if that would ever have been possible.'

'What things?' he prompted, homing in on the detail she'd revealed.

'Oh, nothing terrible. I just mean I've worked at school fairs doing sketch portraits, or markets, I've waitressed and bussed tables, doing whatever I can to earn money, so that I can keep doing what I really love.'

'Which is painting.'

She nodded slowly. 'But I've always known I'd probably have to grow up and get a real job some day.'

'Your talent is rare. You shouldn't abandon your art.' The praise, so casually given, made her stomach roll.

'Thank you. But, talented or not, it's not an easy world to break into.'

He seemed to take her statement and mull on it, thinking it over for a moment, before nodding, almost dismissively. 'I must insist on calling your parents for myself, Frankie.'

'But…why?'

He expelled slowly and his breath fanned her temple, so her blonde hair shifted a little. His eyes lifted to the motion. 'Because there is no excuse for having left you. You were pregnant. Alone. And I should have been there.'

'You didn't know—'

He pressed a finger to her lips, his eyes beseeching her for silence. 'I am not a man to run from his responsibilities.' He was so strong, so big, she felt his insistence and understood it. 'I failed you. I failed Leo. And your parents deserve to hear that from me.'

Frankie was utterly struck dumb. His admission was almost an apology, one she had never expected from him.

'You had no idea about Leo,' she said quietly in an attempt to relieve him of his burden of guilt. 'I know you would have helped me if you had.'

'We would have married,' he agreed with complete confidence, never mind what Frankie might have thought of that. 'And you would never have known a day of worry in your life.'

She silently disagreed with that. Perhaps not financial worry, but emotional? Oh, yes. This marriage was going to be fraught with stress for Frankie.

CHAPTER EIGHT

AFTER A BAKING-HOT DAY, it was bliss to sink into the cool water of the swimming pool and stare out at the glistening sea. Bliss to be alone, with her hair in a simple braid, her face wiped of make-up, her space clear of servants. Leo had thrown a tantrum in the afternoon and though Liana had remained calm and helped Frankie remember that two-year-olds threw tantrums, that there was nothing abnormal about that behaviour, especially in strong-willed little boys, Frankie was nonetheless drained. And it had less to do with Leo and more to do with Matthias than Frankie wanted to admit. Every encounter with the man who would become her husband required so much effort. So much self-control. It was becoming increasingly difficult to remember why she wanted to keep him at arm's length. Or to care.

In the face of her desire for Matthias, sex for sex's sake was a palatable option, even when she'd always believed otherwise. Her need to control this seemed futile and absurd given that they would marry. Wasn't she only fighting to delay the inevitable? Why not just succumb? Why not enjoy what he was offering?

She duck-dived beneath the water's surface and swam a lap, holding her breath until her lungs were stinging, then pushing up off the tiled bottom and resting her elbows on the sun-warmed terracotta tiles.

Frustration gnawed at her—she pushed it aside with effort, focusing on the vista before her. She couldn't imagine a better view from anywhere in the world.

A moment later, she did another lap, then another, then switched to freestyle on the water's surface. She'd been a strong swimmer through school, and she'd always enjoyed it. But nothing was as nice as this. The water in the pool was salty, the twilight sun had the perfect degree of warmth and after the trials of staying calm in the face of Leo's belligerence it was a delight to expend some energy in this way.

Three more laps, and she emerged to find that she was no longer alone. Matthias had slipped into the pool unannounced and, though he stood on the opposite side, he was watching her, and he might as well have reached out and touched her, for how her body reacted to his presence.

'Matt...' she cleared her throat '... I didn't know you were here.'

'I just arrived.'

How did he have the ability to unsettle her with a single look? Her nerves struggled to find harmony in her body.

'I spoke to your father.'

Frankie's eyes flew wide. 'Already?'

He nodded. 'I saw no point in delay.'

'No, of course not. I mean, we're getting married so

soon. I just hadn't expected…' She was babbling. She clamped her lips together and made an effort to focus. 'What did he say?'

'He was pleased for us. I wondered if you might wish to ask them to remain for some time after the wedding, at least to help with Leo while we take our honeymoon.'

'Honeymoon!' The word slid over her back like warmed caramel. She almost groaned at the image it conjured of the two of them, tangled in sheets, warm, passionate, limbs entwined…

'You know, that thing that usually follows a wedding?'

Her cheeks flushed pink. 'But this marriage isn't… I mean… It's not like we need that. Surely you have too much work. Wouldn't it just be an inconvenience?'

'Do you not wish to see more of this country you are to be Queen of?'

She bit down on her lip. 'I just don't think a *honeymoon* is called for.'

'Why do you make the distinction?'

'Honestly? A honeymoon makes me think of beds strewn with rose petals and baths filled with champagne. That's not us.'

'No,' he agreed, moving through the water easily, his long legs carrying him into the deepest part without more than half his chest being submerged. 'But it does not mean we can't have fun.'

Her mouth was dry and every breath of air seemed to make her nerves quiver. 'I think we have different ideas of fun.'

He laughed. 'Do we?'

She flushed and nodded, but her heart was racing, her pulse throbbing. 'I've told you, I'm not interested in casual sex.'

'There's nothing casual about marriage,' he said logically. 'And I think you're very interested in sex with me.'

Her chest squeezed. He closed the distance between them completely and, beneath the water, his long fingers found the edge of her bikini bottoms. With his eyes holding hers, he pulled her close to him. And, damn it, she went, with no resistance whatsoever. As though she were an iron filing and he her magnetic pole.

'Matt,' she murmured as his other hand curved into the bikini bottoms. He was taunting her, his eyes daring her to say something. To tell him to stop. And, though she knew she should, the word wouldn't come out. In fact, nothing came out except a small husky sound of surrender.

'Listen to me,' he said softly, swimming through the water and pulling her with him. He eased her onto one of the steps at the corner of the pool and stood between her legs. 'I want you, and I believe you want me. This—' he gestured from her chest to his '—is like a live wire.'

Her eyes flared at the description; it was exactly how she felt.

Beneath the water, his fingers toyed with the elastic sides of her bikini bottoms, sliding down and curving around her buttocks so she held her breath at the unfamiliar but undeniably welcome contact. She was a fool, she knew—she had to stop this—but oh, it felt so good. Just another minute, she promised herself.

Using his hands to guide her, he brought her body forward a little, so she could feel the strength of his rock-hard arousal, the desire that was there for her, and she whimpered low in her throat. Memories of how he'd felt, moving inside her, made her crazy with longing.

'I am the only man who's ever made love to you. Yes?'

Her cheeks flushed and she shuttered her eyes, unable to meet the scrutiny of his gaze.

'Tell me,' he demanded, kissing her neck so her breath came fast and hard inside her. 'That your only experience of sex is with me.'

A strangled noise escaped her throat. 'Why does it matter?'

'Because if this is so, then you have so much to learn,' he said.

One of his hands moved from her rear, coming over her leg and buzzing the sensitive flesh of her inner thigh, before nudging the flimsy material of her costume aside. She held her breath, her mind no longer able to concentrate on what he'd been saying. He watched her intently as his fingers brushed over her womanhood, his eyes holding hers as he slid a finger into her moist, tight core.

'You have so much to learn about your body and its pleasures, and I want to teach you that.' He swirled his finger around and she arched her back, her eyes fixing on the sunset overhead, on the colours that were only enhanced by the sheer perfection of his touch. 'I want you.' His mouth dropped to the flesh at the base of her throat and he kissed her, slow and long, and she moaned again, wrapping her legs around his waist and surrendering to the bliss of this moment, surrendering to an inevitability she'd been fighting since he'd walked into her gallery and her body had started to feel fully alive for the first time in three years.

'I know you want to fight me—' he rolled his hips and she moaned, his words stoking her like flames in a fire '—but can you not see how good our marriage can be? Neither of us wanted this, but that doesn't mean it can't be everything we want now, Frankie.' Her name on his lips was a seduction, his promise a temptation that was almost impossible to resist. Because he was right. He was so right.

Frankie didn't believe in casual sex, but this wasn't casual. This wasn't even just sex. There was so much more between them; there always had been. At least, for Frankie. He wasn't just some man she'd rushed into bed with. She'd met him and on some level had tripped headlong into love. She'd given all of herself to Matthias that night, not just her virginity. Not just her body.

And he'd walked away with such ease.

Oh, he'd had to—duty had called him. But he'd stayed away and her heart had been breaking.

Could she really lose herself to him again? Could she really be so stupid?

'Tell me you want me,' he said, and he stood out of the pool, removing his hand from her only so he could reach down and lift her, carrying her against his chest as though she weighed nothing.

'I…can't,' she whispered as her hands reached up

and tangled in the hair at his nape, as her body stayed wet and cleaved to his. He carried her to a pool lounger, laying her down and disposing of her bikini bottoms swiftly, staring at her naked sex with eyes that were so hungry they robbed her of breath.

'You can't admit to this?' He arched, kneeling on the ground at the foot of the lounger, parting her thighs with strong, broad hands. His mouth on her was a sensual, terrifying possession and she cried out as pleasure, sharp and visceral, broke through her.

He didn't speak—he didn't need to. His actions made a mockery of her determination not to want him. His tongue ran over her, tasting her sweetness, and his fingers held her legs wide; she was all his. All of her.

She cried out as he moved faster, and then slid a finger deep into her core, tormenting her sensitive nerve-endings with his possession and absolute mastery of her body.

She was so close to breaking point, pleasure within arm's reach, and he lifted his head, his eyes staring at her, his expression impossible to decipher. 'Beg me,' he said simply.

Heat coloured Frankie's mind, cheeks and thoughts.

'Beg me,' he said again, dropping his mouth and lashing her with his tongue once more, his touch like heaven.

'I can't,' she cried, but then his name was dropping from her lips again and again and again, rent with desperate need. She called him Matthias, because here, in this kingdom, beneath the skies of Tolmirós, he was Matthias. Not Matt, who she'd fallen in love with—

she could see that now, looking back through time, and knowing who she'd been then.

At twenty-one, she'd met Matt and fallen in love. But she'd been a girl who believed in fantasies then, who thought sex and love went hand in hand. And now she saw that sex on its own could be enough.

'Beg for me and I will make you come,' he promised, lifting up and taking one of her breasts into his mouth, while his finger stayed inside her, tormenting her with memories and promises.

'Why are you doing this?' she asked, digging her nails into his shoulders as thought became impossible, as pleasure crashed over her. *Surrender*, her body begged, her heart implored. *Surrender and accept that this is enough!*

Of course it was—for some people.

But not for Frankie.

Her body was on fire, her pulse racing, her heart thumping, and she knew that satisfaction was within reach. All she had to do was beg him, to say the word *please* that she was swallowing inside her throat, and he would drive her over the edge; he would make her feel almost whole.

Almost.

But it would never be enough for the girl who'd wanted real love all her life.

'I can't,' she said, her breathing so rushed, dragged from so deep within her lungs it hurt. 'Don't make me beg.'

Surprise covered his features when he pulled up to look at her.

'Don't use what I feel to demean me,' she said, lying flat on the lounger, staring up at the evening streaked sky.

'Demean you?' he repeated, the word ragged. 'Frankie, by getting you to accept what you want, I am empowering you. Empowering you to enjoy sex, to enjoy this thing between us that is purely good. I have no interest in demeaning you. I want you to be brave, to face up to what you're feeling. Stop hiding from me.' And his eyes held hers for a long moment as his mouth dropped closer to her sex. She held her breath, propping up on elbows to watch him.

'Let us try it another way,' he said, the words deep and husky. 'Let me beg you. Let me beg you to let me do this,' and he flicked his tongue out, teasing her flesh so she made a keening sound of pleasure. 'Let me beg and you say, simply, "Yes".'

Yes.

The word was heavy in her throat, bouncing over and over, begging to be said, begging her to agree, so she could be put out of her misery.

'Just say yes,' he repeated, and his mouth moved faster and her pleasure built until her eyes were filled with a bright white light and she was no longer conscious of anything but this.

'Say yes,' he demanded, pulling her body closer so he could go deeper, his mouth possessing her in a way that was so intimate, so personal, so perfect. His hand scooped under her bottom, lifting her up, and she heard herself crying out, over and over and over, giving away a part of her soul that she had thought she would be able to keep locked up: 'Yes, Matthias, please. Please!'

He stared at the painting, his lips a grim slash on his face. *Don't use what I feel to demean me.*

Her words, issued in the heat of a sensual moment of passion, had stuck with him, chasing themselves around his head until he could barely think, until he couldn't fathom what he'd been thinking.

Don't use what I feel to demean me.

Had he been doing that?

Since she'd arrived in Tolmirós, he'd been intent on seducing her, on forcing her to stop hiding from the magnitude of their desire.

Matthias, with his experience of women and sex and attraction, knew what he shared with Frankie was rare. So rare that even three years after their first encounter he hadn't been able to put her from his mind. Three years later and he'd never met anyone who held the same appeal for him. This passion was rare and it deserved to be explored.

But at the cost of her self-esteem?

He swore under his breath, pacing to the windows that overlooked the ocean. It had all seemed so simple when first they'd arrived. Sex was a simple transaction. A conversion of lust to satiation.

Whatever his attitudes were to it, Frankie's were not the same.

And yet he'd driven his tongue over her, tasting her release, delighting in her complete surrender even when he now suspected he should have stopped. He'd thought he would feel triumph with her surrender; he'd thought he'd revel in her total acceptance of the tug of their mutual need.

He hadn't.

He'd felt only something very close to blinding panic. He'd tasted her as she'd fallen apart, and his own body had been begging him to bury his length inside her soft, welcoming core, yet he hadn't. He'd pulled away from her even when her desire had burst around them, and her willingness to succumb to pleasure had been palpable.

He'd been as beholden to passion as she, in the end, but it didn't matter. Because she'd been right. He'd been determined to get her to face what they felt for one another.

But why?

Why did he care so damned much that she should surrender to this desire?

Because he wanted her. He wanted her with the strength of a thousand stars, and he knew she felt the same. But her determination and willpower were many times stronger than his. Why? What did she want? Not just from him, but in general?

The damned fairy tale? He couldn't offer that. He didn't have it within his power to give Frankie the dream of love and happily ever after. But he could give her more than sex. He could give her enough, surely, to make her truly happy—not just in bed but as his wife?

And he wanted her to be happy, he admitted to himself now. He needed her to be happy, to smile at him as she had on those few rare occasions since coming to

Tolmirós. He wanted to win her trust, to *earn* her trust, and the rest, surely, would follow.

Maybe it wouldn't. But Frankie deserved more than to have a husband who wanted only her body. She deserved as much of the dream as he could offer—surely some of her fantasy would be better than none?

'You look like a little prince,' Frankie enthused, tears sparkling on her lashes as she studied her son. He'd undergone a similar makeover to her own: a haircut, new clothes, and he looked utterly divine.

''E is so handsome. Just like his father,' Liana cooed, her eyes wrinkling at the corners as she bent down and picked Leo up. He didn't arch his back with Liana in the way he'd taken to doing with Frankie, she noticed with a wry grimace. Liana always got hugs and kisses and yeses straight away. But Frankie couldn't be cross about that—not when Liana had helped make Leo's transition to life in Tolmirós so easy.

A whisper of guilt flicked through her because there were only days to go until the wedding and though Frankie had spent her days ensuring Leo was settling well and making sure this private residence of the palace felt like home, she was distracted almost all the time.

When she'd first agreed to this, he'd told her two things. *Through the days, you'll barely know I exist. At night, you won't be able to exist without me.*

The latter was true. Since the afternoon in the pool, when she had surrendered herself to his mouth and given up her determination to resist the passion that flared between them, he'd made no effort to touch her. He'd come to bed late and lay on his side until he'd fallen asleep, and she'd lifted her head up and watched him, and flopped onto her back and wondered what he'd say if she gave into all her body's urges and straddled him, and begged him to forget what she'd said: to make love to her.

As for the days, she more than knew he existed then too.

He was everywhere she looked in this palace. He was in their son's face, Liana's pride, his servants' obedience, the kingdom's prosperity. He was in the enormous canary diamond and white gold ring he'd slid onto her finger two nights earlier, his eyes locked onto hers as he told her it reminded him of the yellow she'd painted the sunlight in the painting she'd been working on the weekend they'd met. And though it was a meaningless, throwaway comment, it had made her chest feel as if it were exploding with delirious joy, with pleasure and disbelief. With perfection.

He was everywhere, even when he'd said he wouldn't be, even when he made no effort to seduce her. Their conversations were polite, cordial, and lacking any indication that he even wanted her. Perhaps he didn't. Perhaps it was as simple as an impulse for him—she'd told him 'no' and he'd accepted that. If only Frankie had found it so easy to put him from her mind!

'Thank you for getting him ready for tonight, Liana, and for agreeing to come.'

'Of course! My place is with him at these functions—as much as you would like me to be,' she added tactfully. 'Royal parties are not much fun for children. They tire so quickly of being polite and well-behaved.' She looked at Leo with a wink and then reached into her pocket, pulling out a small round chocolate. 'And Leo knows there will be a treat at the end of the night, for his very good behaviour.'

Leo nodded sagely, and Frankie laughed. 'Is this his prince face?' she suggested, pride bursting through her.

'He has been practising.'

'Well, Leo, you've absolutely mastered it.'

Liana turned to face Frankie and, for the first time, looked at her properly. 'You are very beautiful, Frankie. Like a princess yourself, no?'

'Oh, no, but thank you,' she demurred, feeling more like someone going to a dressing up party. 'Ball gowns aren't really my caper.'

'Caper?' Liana frowned.

'Thing. They're not really my thing.' She ran her hands down the dress, a turquoise colour, it had a sweetheart neckline and was fitted to her waist, then fell into a flouncy skirt that made a beautiful swishing sound as she walked. It was a true Cinderella dress and the diamond tiara that had been styled into her hair completed the look. 'The dress is very beautiful, though.'

'It does suit you,' Liana complimented.

'Well, that's good, because I get the feeling I'm going to need to go to a few more of these things in my lifetime.' She shrugged her slender shoulders, her tan golden. She'd taken to spending time by the pool as well. Helping Leo swim, and swimming with him, lying in the sun while he napped, remembering how

Matthias had felt in the water, how warm and cool had contrasted so sensually against her flesh.

Her cheeks flushed pink as the memories pushed into her mind and then, as if she'd somehow miraculously dredged him up from fantasy to reality, Matthias strode into the room.

If she looked like a princess, then he was King Charming come to life.

The suit was jet black, his shirt whiter than white, a white tie at his neck completed the look. But he wore across his middle a burgundy sash, military style medals were pinned to his chest, and at his waist there was a gold weapon, a blade, long and sharp. He was far more handsome than any man had a right to be.

'Sword!' Leo pointed delightedly and he jumped up off his little bottom and held his hands out, so Matthias smiled at Liana and then took his son into his arms, tousling hair that had, a moment ago, been perfectly neat.

She didn't notice the way Matthias's eyes lingered on Leo's face with a hint of something other than happiness; she didn't see the way his expression flashed with regret and—oh, so briefly—fear.

'Sword,' Leo said again and Matthias relaxed, smiling as he nodded.

'Yes.'

'For me?'

Liana laughed, and Matthias pulled a face. 'Not yet. But soon.'

Leo pouted. 'I see?'

Matthias put their son down on the ground and then removed the clip from his waist. He held the sword—in its gold ceremonial sheath—so that Leo could run his fingertips over the blunted end.

'Look, Mama. Pictures.'

At this, Matthias glanced up, his eyes locking onto Frankie's, holding hers, and a look of searing heat flashed between them—a look that had the ability to blank anyone else from their presence. Her fingers fidgeted at her sides and then she smiled curtly, tightly, in a way that didn't feel natural and dragged her eyes down to the sword.

But desire stayed lodged in her chest, desperate, hungry, craving indulgence. Out of nowhere, she remembered the way his mouth had felt between her legs and her knees almost buckled with the sensual heat of her recollection.

'I see,' she murmured, moving closer.

'It's very old,' Matthias said, turning his attention back to the weapon. 'It was my great-great-great-great-great-grandfather's, said to have slain the king of a neighbouring country when war threatened at our doorstep.'

'War?' Leo was fascinated by this.

'A long time ago,' Frankie jumped in, sending a warning look to Matthias. He smiled at her and a dimple formed in his cheek that made her fingers itch to paint him. She had in her mind, so many times.

He stood, unfurling his body length and ruffling Leo's dark hair at the same time. 'You look beautiful.' The words were quietly spoken, intended purely for her ears.

'Thank you,' she said, able to take the compliment

when she felt her appearance was really the result of couture and hair stylists.

'But not complete yet.'

She looked down at the dress and lifted a hand to the diamond choker she wore. 'What have I forgotten?'

His smile was enigmatic as he reached into his pocket and pulled out a rectangular velvet box.

'Would you do me the honour of wearing this to-night, Frankie?' He popped it open to reveal an award similar to those he wore—a thick piece of purple fabric to which a small gold pendant was attached. In the centre of the pendant there was a star, with an arrow striking through it.

'What is it?' she asked, watching as he pulled it from the box. His fingers were deft and confident, and her mouth was suddenly dry.

'The Star of Aranathi,' he said. 'An award that was given to my mother—one of my country's highest.'

The meaningfulness of the gesture touched something in Frankie's stomach, and it set in place a chain reaction. Butterflies stirred to life, slowly at first, then faster, until a whole kaleidoscope was beating against her insides. She was oblivious to the watchful eyes of Liana, who'd moved Leo away and distracted him with a juice carton.

'What's it for?' she murmured. He lifted the ribbon to the top of her dress, his fingers almost clinical as they held the fabric taut enough to thread the pin through and latch it into place.

'Humanitarian efforts.'

'I don't...' Frankie frowned, studying Matthias up

close. She studied him not as a woman who wanted a man, but as an artist evaluating a subject. She measured his features and imagined creating him from the nothingness of canvas and pigment. She imagined how she might mix her colours together to shade the cleft of his chin dimple and the very faint darkness beneath his eyes. It was his lashes, though, that fascinated her. They were black and curling, soft like silk and so thick, as though they were a curtain for his eyes. What of his face had been gifted by his mother, and what by his father?

When she looked at Leo, she saw so much of Matthias. But was some of the Queen there too? The Queen to whom this medal had once belonged?

'I don't know anything about her,' Frankie finished after a moment. 'But I'd like to.'

His expression shifted with pride first, and then surprise. 'Why?'

Frankie tilted her head consideringly. 'Because she was your mother. And Leo's grandmother. And it strikes me that I should know something about your family, beyond the fact…' The sentence trailed off into nothingness as she realised what she'd been about to say.

'That they're dead,' he finished for her, his expression unchanged. She threw a scant look in Leo's direction; the boy wasn't listening. Nonetheless, Frankie's brows knitted together when she regarded Matthias. She'd prefer to handle that conversation sensitively, when it came time for Leo to learn of his father's family's deaths.

'What did your mother do to receive this award?'

'Many things.'

'War!' Frankie startled as Leo seemed to jolt out of his reverie and, from the other side of the room, whipped the straw from the juice carton and held it towards Matthias like an ancient challenge to a duel.

Matthias's face relaxed, the tension of a moment ago dissipating, his eyes crinkling at the corners as he returned, *'En garde!'*

Leo giggled and charged his father, but Matthias caught him mid-run, lifting him up easily and tickling him at the belly, so Leo's laughter pealed into the room and, before she knew it, Frankie was smiling. But it was a distracted smile, a smile that was only skin-deep.

'Excuse me, Your Majesty.' There was a knock at the door. 'It is time.'

'Of course.' Leo's smile muted itself when he addressed the servant, and Frankie saw in that moment the duality between private and public. The man and the King. The man who could smile and laugh and tease their son about long ago wars, and the King who presented a sombre and considered face to his servants at all times.

Had he been like that at fifteen? Or had he been allowed to mourn?

They were to be married in the Artheki Cathedrali, her secretary had informed her days earlier. It was five miles away, ancient, and all the Kings of Tolmirós had been married, christened and mourned within its walls for over a thousand years. That information had been inserted into the briefing and, though it was an unimportant detail, it had played on Frankie's mind.

She presumed then that Matthias's parents and

brother had been buried there, that their funeral had taken place within the walls of the cathedral at which they were to marry. Had he spoken at the funeral? At fifteen years old, it wouldn't have been unusual, but her heart broke to imagine the young boy he'd been, and the pressure that must have been upon him.

She resisted the temptation to run an Internet search on the subject. Her curiosity was natural, but she would prefer her information to come from the source. Snooping around and reading articles online felt somehow wrong.

'Come, *deliciae.*' Was she imagining the way his voice caught as he addressed her? The way his eyes seemed to lock onto hers with emotion and an intent she couldn't comprehend? 'It is time for you to meet our people.'

CHAPTER NINE

'Oh, Matthias!' They were alone in a sleek dark limousine, with Liana and Leo following in the car behind. 'It's so beautiful.'

Beyond the black tinted windows of the car and the crowds that had lined the streets hoping for a real-life glimpse of the soon-to-be Queen, Frankie could see the streets of Tolmirós and they were setting her soul on fire.

'It's like something out of a beautiful story book. I had no idea!' Terracotta-roofed houses, built close together and higgledy-piggledy, one leaning this way and the next the other, were all washed in different colours of pastel paints. Little balconies had wrought-iron details and window boxes overflowing with bright purple and red plants. Many had refused to be contained to the small pots and were making joyous bids for sunshine and freedom, dancing their tendrils down the sides of the buildings, forming veins of green that shone in the late afternoon sun.

But the most remarkable thing to Frankie was the sense of history that was at every turn. These buildings were ancient. They whooshed past a church with a cupola and a bell tower, white with a shimmering blue face and enormous bronze hands. A statue of a naked man stood in front, and geraniums seemed to grow with complete abandon across a side wall. When she turned in her seat to get a better look, she saw a nun coming from the front gates, throwing something towards the ground. A moment later at least a hundred pigeons descended on the square. The nun threw her head back and laughed and then the limousine turned the corner.

Caught up in the wonderment of this picture-book streetscape, Frankie didn't realise that Matthias was watching her intently. She didn't see the way his eyes were scanning her face, reading every flicker of delight that crossed it.

'I had no idea it would be like this.'

His lips quirked. 'What did you expect?'

Frankie shrugged. 'I guess I didn't think about it. Until a week ago, Tolmirós was just some place on the edge of the Mediterranean. And since we arrived, we've been in the palace. I expected beautiful beaches and, I guess, a modern city, but this is…just…stunning.'

Pride flashed on his features and his nod was swift. 'The city of Novampoli was built in the nineteen-seventies. We needed a place that wasn't part of the port cities—much of our prosperity comes from being a safe harbour for shipping companies, but my father kick-started a technology revolution. Banking and finance are also primary industries for Tolmirós. We needed a city that would answer those requirements. The first few buildings were modest but within a decade or two high-rises began to shape the skyline. It is now a place of glass and steel, and the food there is second to none. I will take you there, when next I have occasion to go. You will like it.'

'Is it like Manhattan?' She settled back into her seat, smoothing the skirts of her dress simply for something to do with her hands.

'In some ways, but without the mix of old and new. It is more like Dubai, I think. A somewhat artificial-seeming city, in a place you wouldn't expect it. The whole island is a city, and an enormous bridge spans from the west shore to its neighbouring island, Emanakki.'

'I'd like to see it some day,' she said with a smile. 'I want to see everything.'

He laughed softly. 'And so you shall, Frankie. In fact, soon it will be your duty to see and know everything about our country.'

She angled him a look thoughtfully. 'Who were you going to marry?'

He arched a brow at her change in conversation. 'That seems irrelevant now.'

'I'm curious. Indulge me.'

'I think I told you that I hadn't yet decided…'

Feminine disapproval had her lips curling. 'Of course. You had a queen *smorgasbord* from which to se-lect your bride. I'm just asking who it was likely to be.'

He smothered a smile at her comment and nodded. 'Lady Tianna Montavaigne was the front-runner.'

'Why?'

'She met the criteria.' He shrugged, as though it barely mattered.

But Frankie was persistent. 'In what ways?'

He compressed his lips and studied her for a long moment, his eyes tunnelling straight into her soul. 'She's royal, for one, though a distant cousin to the ruling monarch of Sweden. She's been raised to understand this lifestyle, the pressures of it, the need to be discreet, polite, dignified and private. She understands the realities of living life under a microscope.' He said the final sentence with a hint of disdain, but it was gone again almost as quickly. 'She is intelligent, beautiful, and we get on well.'

There was a pang of something in the region of Frankie's heart. 'Will she be disappointed not to marry you? Did she love you?'

He laughed and shook his head ruefully. 'It is always about love with you, no?'

Frankie's cheeks warmed as his eyes held hers thoughtfully. 'No, she doesn't *love* me.'

Frankie sighed softly. 'You act as though the very idea of marriage between two people who are in love is absurd.'

'Not absurd,' he contradicted. 'Just…romantic. Tianna knew what marriage to me would involve.'

'I just can't understand why anyone would agree to that,' she said with a shake of her head. 'A marriage without love seems so…cold. So…devastating.' She shivered.

'*You* have agreed to it,' he pointed out, watching her through half-shuttered eyes.

Her eyes flashed with pain and then she tilted her chin as though physically underscoring her determination.

'I… I know. But our circumstances are fairly unique. Were there no Leo, wild horses couldn't have dragged me into this.'

He nodded, as though her words were somehow reassuring. 'Tianna is in a relationship with her father's chauffeur. He's from Syria and came to the country as a refugee when he was a child. He's naturalised now, and she cares for him very deeply.'

Frankie blinked, her lack of comprehension apparent. 'So why in the world would she marry you?'

'Because he needs his job, because her parents would never condone the match, because she'd be disinherited and doesn't particularly fancy the idea of getting a job. There are any number of reasons to keep their relationship quiet. Marriage to me would have provided excellent cover for her to continue her relationship.'

'Oh, Matt, how can you speak so calmly about this?'

He sighed and squeezed her hand. 'I can't see there's anything wrong with making informed, intelligent choices when it comes to your future.'

The car began to slow, and the crowds outside their windows thickened. Frankie had been given a crash course in royal deportment. For hours each morning and again in the evening, she'd been drilled in the protocol that would be expected of her as the future Queen. It all jumbled in her brain now, but she tried to grab hold of it.

'Relax,' he murmured, leaning closer to look out at the view with her. 'The window will go down soon so you can wave to my people. They're excited to see you.'

Beyond the window, now that they were driving more slowly, Frankie could see signs with their official engagement portrait, taken on the balcony of the palace, her head pressed against Matthias's chest. There were handmade signs too, with her name all over them, and people wearing veils and throwing confetti.

Was Leo enjoying the spectacle? Or was he frightened by the noise? She angled herself in the seat in an attempt to look backwards but the limo was a little far away. 'Why aren't Leo and Liana in this car? There's plenty of room.'

He didn't look at her. 'In case something goes wrong.'

'Like what? He's never motion sick. He travels well…' Her voice tapered off as an alternative meaning unravelled in her brain. 'You mean in case our car crashes?'

He shrugged. 'Or theirs does. Or there's a terrorist attack.'

'So you won't ever travel with our son?'

He eyed her now, his expression implacable. 'No.'

'But you flew over here with him.'

He nodded. 'It was necessary on that one occasion. But I will not do so again. I have had this law written into our constitution.'

A shiver ran down her spine, and her chest heaved with emotion for the young man who'd felt it necessary to write in such a protection.

Surely this was a reaction to the loss of his parents and brother. She couldn't help it; she reached over and squeezed his hand, rubbing the pad of her thumb reassuringly over his skin. But he looked at her with a quizzical expression, and Frankie realised her eyes were moist. Emotions were running rampant within her.

'Surely that's a little extreme?'

His features were like ice. 'No.'

'But he's just a baby,' she murmured. 'He'd much rather travel with his mother or father.'

'He is my heir,' Matthias said through clenched teeth. 'Keeping him alive is my priority.'

She ignored the unpleasant suspicion he was speaking as a king who needed a living heir rather than a father who valued the survival of his child. Of course it was both. 'Then I'll travel with him in the future,' she said simply.

'Your place is with me,' he rebuffed gently, his eyes sweeping closed for a moment. 'And Liana is there for Leo.'

'You created this law,' she prompted softly, gently. 'So there wasn't one before this?'

His eyes fired. 'No. If there had been…' The words trailed off into nothing and now she was moving closer to him, needing him to hear her.

'If there had been,' she insisted, 'that boulder would have still been there. The car with your parents in would have crashed.'

'But Spiro would have lived.' His eyes glittered with hurt and pain and her heart twisted achingly.

'You don't know that,' she whispered softly. 'You don't know that your car wouldn't have crashed as well. You don't know that something else awful might not have happened later. There are no guarantees in life,' she said simply.

'You think I don't know that?' He turned to face her, his expression tortured, his features drawn. 'You think

I don't understand how completely beholden we are to fate and sheer damned luck?'

His hurt was like a rock, pressing against her chest. 'So stop trying to control everything,' she murmured, lifting a hand to his cheek. 'I don't want our son growing up afraid of his own shadow. I don't want him being governed by protocols and edicts that overturn natural instinct. He's our son. He belongs with us.'

She pressed her head forward, so their foreheads connected, and she breathed in deeply, this connection somehow every bit as intimate as what they'd shared by the pool.

'It's my responsibility to protect you both, and I will do so with my dying breath.' The words shook with the force of his determination, and Frankie was momentarily speechless.

Then, with a surge of understanding, she cupped his cheek, holding him still. 'Is that what this is about? You think you couldn't save Spiro and now you're trying to guarantee that nothing bad will ever happen to us?' Her insight was blinding in its strength and accuracy. She knew she was right when he recoiled for a moment. But she moved with him, staying close, holding him to her. 'You were just a boy, Matthias. You couldn't do any more than you did.'

'How do you know?' he asked, uncharacteristically weary. 'You weren't there. You don't know anything about the accident…'

'I know that if you could have saved your brother or your parents, you would have. I know that if there's anyone on earth with the strength to almost make the impossible possible, it's you, Matt. You have to forgive yourself. Free yourself from this guilt.'

'Easier said than done.' He expelled a sigh and shook his head. 'I will not change my mind about Leo's safety. You'll have to respect that I know what I'm talking about.' He was himself again. Matthias Vassiliás—a king amongst men, intractable, unchangeable, determined. The emotionally charged air was gone and he sat back in his seat as if to say, *conversation closed.*

Frankie was about to argue with him, she wanted, desperately, to alleviate this guilt of his, but the windows began to move down slowly and she had only seconds to sit back in her seat and compose her features into an expression of assumed happiness, lift her hand and begin to wave slowly at the assembled crowds. The noise was deafening! People began to scream when the window went down, loud and shrill, but oh, so excited. The crowd applauded and children threw flowers at the car.

The conversation with Matthias pushed deeper into her mind, for later analysis, in the face of such a rapturous welcome. Matthias, beside her, seemed unaffected. He didn't smile nor wave, but simply watched Frankie and allowed her to have all the adoration of the people who'd come to see the woman who would be Queen.

She was so captivated by the crowds that she didn't notice the castle until they were almost on top of it but, as the car slowed to a stop, she glanced up and an involuntary rush of breath escaped her. 'Oh, Matt, look!'

His smile was just a flicker. 'I know.'

It was an ancient-looking castle, with enormous turrets that were topped with pointed roofs. As a child she'd read a book about Sir Gawain and she'd always imagined the castle to be something like this.

'It was the palace of a prominent family in the twelfth century. As civil wars gradually broke down the ranks of nobility, the palace reverted to the Crown. It serves as our parliament, and the west wing is used as a gallery for children to come and learn about the country's politics.

'I've never seen anything like it.' Windows had been set in ancient brick, the glass rippled and uneven, showing its age.

'You should see it from the other side,' he teased but, before she could ask him what he meant, the doors were opened by a guard in a full liveried uniform and white gloves. The crowd reached a deafening pitch. Frankie moved towards the door but Matthias stilled her, holding her back in the limousine, safe from prying eyes for one more moment.

'Do you feel okay?'

She frowned. 'I feel…fine. Why?'

'This could be overwhelming. Do you need anything?'

His thoughtfulness, so unexpected, made her stomach swoop as though she'd fallen from an aeroplane. 'I'm honestly fine,' she promised. 'Really, I am.'

He nodded, a glint of admiration in his eyes as he released her hand. Remembering all that she'd been taught, she stepped from the car, concentrating on keeping her long skirt down for modesty, her head up, her eyes on the crowd, no dramatic facial movements that a camera would snap and a paper would publish for the fact it was unflattering. She also concentrated doubly hard on not falling flat on her face, which was harder than it sounded whilst wearing stiletto heels and what felt like miles of tulle and silk.

She'd been told they weren't to hold hands, nor to show any sign of affection. It was a protocol thing and, given their strange and somewhat dysfunctional relationship, she hadn't blinked at the instruction. So when he stepped from the car and put an arm around her waist, holding her to his side, she glanced up at him.

He smiled brightly, his even white teeth set in curving lips, a chiselled square jawline and every feature a stand-out, his dark eyes casting a spell over her, and she smiled back at him. Then he bent down and pressed a small kiss to the tip of her nose. The crowd went wild.

He lifted his head up but kept an arm wrapped around her waist in a way that she would have called protective, except the flames of desire that licked at her side were so much more dangerous than any other threat or fear she might feel.

He guided her to the crowds and she received gifts from the children who were lined up at the front. Dozens and dozens of cards, flowers, bears, and each one she admired and appreciated, before handing it to a protocol officer, hovering in the background. At the steps of the palace, Leo and Liana met them, having pulled up and made their way straight to the entrance.

Liana straightened Leo's shirt and then passed him to Matthias. With their son held in one handsome arm and the other around the waist of the woman he would marry, they stood there, smiling at the assembled crowd.

The smile on Frankie's face was dazzling, but it was a forgery.

Sadness for this man swarmed her chest, making her heart split and her mind heavy. She didn't want him to have suffered as he had. She saw now the depth of his grief—it was as much a part of him as his bones and blood. It had redefined his outlook on life. And love?

Matthias tilted his head towards her and it felt as though an elastic band was snapping inside her chest, her heart exploding out of its bracket.

He might not love her—he might not even be capable of love.

But if her sense of compassion for him taught Frankie anything it was that somewhere, somehow, without her permission, she'd done something really stupid.

She'd fallen in love with her future husband.

If the outside of the palace was mesmerising, then inside was just as much so. Enormous marble tiles lay in the entranceway, white and imposing, and a marble staircase rose from the centre. A harpist was playing as they strode inside, and more noise sounded, this time from within the palace. 'The party is on the rooftop terrace,' he said.

'Okay.' She nodded, but her mind was still exploding from the realisation she'd just had. She *couldn't* love him. No way. She was, surely, just getting lust and love mixed up, as she had back in New York. She barely knew him.

Yet somewhere along the way she'd fallen in love

with a man who'd proudly proclaimed his disdain for the whole notion of love. He saw it as a useless impediment to life in general.

What a fool she was!

'You are okay?' he queried again, carrying Leo on his hip as though he'd been doing it all Leo's life.

'Uh huh.' She nodded unevenly, not daring to look at him again.

'Please, Frankie, do not be worried about Leo's safety. I will protect him, and you.'

She jolted her gaze to his, nodding. If only he knew what the real cause for her silence was!

They walked up the sweeping staircase in silence. She realised as they neared the top that Matthias had been right about something—she now barely noticed the servants that were standing on every second step, all dressed in formal military uniforms.

At the top landing, four guards stood, two on either side of enormous wide wooden doors, each carved with striking scenes that she'd have loved to have stood and studied. The doors themselves looked ancient.

As the family approached, the guards bowed low then saluted, all in perfect time with one another.

'Police!' Leo squealed, and one of the four guards lost control of his stern expression for the briefest of seconds, relaxing his lips into a spontaneous smile before focusing himself.

The tallest of the men took a large gold sceptre and banged it slowly three times against the wooden doors; they then swept inwards as if by magic.

The terrace, though filled with hundreds of people,

was absolutely silent, and space had been left in the middle of the assembly—a corridor of sorts.

With his arm around her waist once more, Matthias guided Frankie forward. The group of people was silent. Frankie and Matthias were silent.

Leo was not.

'People!' he exclaimed gleefully, clapping his hand together. 'Lots and lots of people, Mama!' And everyone laughed, so Leo laughed, and then lifted his chubby little hands to cover his eyes for a moment before pulling them away and saying, 'Boo!'

More laughter, from Frankie too, who looked up helplessly at Matthias.

'And I worried he might feel nervous,' Matthias murmured from the side of his mouth.

'Apparently we have a showman on our hands,' she agreed, as Leo played peek-a-boo once more with the delighted crowd.

Conversation began to return to normal and, without the eyes of the world on them, Frankie looked around the terrace more thoroughly. It was then that she noticed something at first familiar and at second glance jarring.

'My paintings are here.' She was dumbfounded. For, hanging on the far wall of the palace, were some of her paintings. The sun was setting and it bathed them in the most beautiful natural light. She stared at the artworks with a growing sense of confusion. 'How in the world…?'

His look gave nothing away. 'You can no longer sell your paintings, Frankie. It wouldn't be appropriate. But that doesn't mean the world should be deprived of your talent.'

'I…but you…these were supposed to be showing in New York.'

He nodded. 'I bought the whole lot.'

'You bought…'

'It wouldn't have been appropriate for the show to go ahead, with news of our engagement.'

'But why buy them? If you'd said that, I would have called Charles and explained…'

'And deprived him of his commission?' He shook his head. 'He picked you to show your work; he is obviously very good at what he does. Why shouldn't he earn a reward for that?'

His perceptiveness and flattery pinballed inside her. 'I had no idea…'

'This was my intention.'

Hope flew in her chest, because the gesture was so sweet, so kind, so utterly out of left field. 'Thank you,' she said after several long seconds, as Liana approached. 'I'm truly touched.'

And, as if sensing that she might be at risk of reading too much into it, he straightened. 'It was simply the right thing to do, Frankie. Your art deserves to be seen, you cannot sell it any longer, or it would be seen that you are profiteering from your position as Queen. And this is now your country—of course the works should hang here, in Tolmirós.'

It was all so businesslike and sensible, but that didn't completely take the shine off the gesture. Because she found it almost impossible to believe that only pragmatism and common sense had motivated it. Surely, there was a thread of something else, something more?

He praised her artwork, but her artwork was *her*. Every painting was a construct of her soul, a creation of her being. To like it, to appreciate it, was to appreciate her.

'Come, *deliciae*, everybody here is eager to meet you. I hope you're not tired.'

He led her towards the Prime Minister first and for the next three hours Frankie met and spoke to more people than she could ever remember.

Matthias stayed by her side the whole time, intensely watchful, an arm around her waist at all times, shooting arrows of desire deep within her, his body warm, his eyes never leaving her.

When it came time for them to exit she was exhausted, but the fluttering of hope inside her heart refused to die down.

In a week she would marry the man she'd fallen in love with, and she refused to believe there was no hope that he would, one day, love her right back. He'd put his heart on ice, and who could blame him? He'd suffered an intense loss, a total tragedy, so he'd put his heart on ice…and Frankie was determined that she would thaw it.

CHAPTER TEN

'YOU DID WELL TONIGHT.' He watched as she strolled into their bedroom wearing a silk negligee that fell to the floor. All night he'd watched her, and he'd ignored every damned royal protocol, keeping an arm clamped vice-like around her waist because he couldn't *not* touch her. The urge had surprised the hell out of him.

At first, he'd wanted to reassure her, to protect her, just as he'd said in the car. Though she'd promised him she was fine with the event, the crowds and the attention, he'd felt she was nervous. He'd felt her energy and he'd wanted to soothe her worries. Then, when they'd stepped onto the terrace and she'd begun to charm her way around his parliament, speaking in halting Tol-mirón that she'd been learning since arriving in the country, he'd felt something else. Something dark and sinister and distinctly unwelcome.

Jealousy.

He hadn't wished to share Frankie.

Every single person had wanted some of her time and attention and Frankie was so generous and giving that she would have obliged for another three hours, if he hadn't called an end to the evening with his speech. Even as he'd given the closing words he'd watched her— watched the way she stood, the way the evening wind rustled past her hair, catching it and pulling it out to- wards the sea, as though the wind and the ocean knew that she really did belong here in Tolmirós.

His eyes narrowed at the intensity of his thoughts, the depth of his feelings, and he suppressed them with determination.

'I had fun,' she said simply. 'It turns out I'm quite the attention-seeker.'

He lifted a brow but whatever response he'd been about to make fell out of his brain as she lifted her arms and began to style her hair. Long and waved, she lifted it onto her head into a messy bun, and the movement thrust her breasts forward, her nipples erect beneath the pale silk of the nightgown.

Oblivious to his heated inspection, she continued, 'You might have created a monster.'

He recognised that he had—but it was not the mon- ster of which Frankie spoke. Matthias was in very real danger of becoming obsessed with Frankie.

Again.

But so much worse this time. He wanted her. All day and all night, his body craved her with a single- mindedness that he hadn't felt since he was a teen- ager and first learning the ways of his body's sensual needs. But tonight had shown him it was more than that. He didn't want anyone else to claim her attention. He didn't want her to talk and laugh and commiserate with *anyone*.

She'd spoken of her childhood and he'd listened, resenting the fact that she was sharing details he didn't know with a stranger.

There was danger in all those feelings and he rejected them, knowing they were not a part of his life, knowing he didn't welcome them.

'I'm kidding,' she said, and now she was looking at him, a quizzical expression on her brow. 'I just meant it wasn't as scary as I thought it would be.'

He nodded, eyes watchful. 'You're a natural.'

'Do you really think so?'

Her doubts opened vulnerability inside his chest like a chasm—a desire to shield her from ever feeling uncertain. He ignored the need to reassure her, to pepper her with praise and compliments and fill her with confidence in herself. For promises were inherent in that and he didn't want to make promises to Frankie when he had no idea of how to keep them.

'Yes.' He spoke the word like a whip cracking into the room. 'And you will have a busy week of such engagements.'

'Oh?'

'In the days before the wedding, diplomats and dignitaries will arrive to pay their respects to the woman who will be Queen. You will have many appointments.'

'I see.' She nodded thoughtfully. 'I remember.'

'You are not worried about it?'

'Well, I wish I had a better grasp on Tolmirón,' she said pragmatically, 'but, other than that, no. I'm not shy, Matthias. I have no issue talking to strangers.'

She dropped her hands to her sides and smiled brightly—Matthias's gut rolled. 'I saw that tonight.'

Her smile dropped. Damn it, the words had sounded critical, his jealousy not something he was able to disguise.

'But that's a good thing?'

His eyes narrowed. She poured herself a glass of water from the crystal decanter across the room and sipped it.

'Yes,' he said gruffly, finally, unable to take his eyes off her.

She padded across the room, so graceful and lithe. It was a warm night and the windows were open, so the hint of the ocean's fragrance was carried to them on the breeze. She climbed into bed, sitting up rather than lying down. His fingers itched to reach out and touch her—the smooth, tanned skin of her arms drew his gaze.

'People are in awe of you,' she observed, tilting her head to look at him.

He shrugged lightly. 'I'm their King.'

'Yes, I know.' She seemed to be mulling that over. 'And tonight you seemed like it.'

'As opposed to?'

'Being King is so much a part of you. I guess I still find it hard to understand why you didn't tell me who you are. What you are. Three years ago. In New York,' she added, as if he didn't know exactly what she meant.

'It was a novelty to meet someone who didn't know,' he said truthfully. 'And I discovered I liked being treated like any other man.'

'Not like any other man,' she said, so softly the words

were almost carried away towards the open window, then her ocean-green eyes latched onto his. Something pulled inside him. 'You weren't like any man I'd ever, ever met.'

He dismissed the words, refusing to let them matter to him.

'I mean it,' she said softly, her words reaching deep into his chest. 'You were so overwhelming.'

Her eyes held his, studying him in that way she had, as though she were pulling him apart piece by piece, and weighing every fragment of him in her hands. 'That's lust,' he dismissed. 'Desire.' And to prove his point he caught her hand and brought it to his lips, pressing a light kiss to her racing pulse point there. His eyes held hers as he moved his mouth to her palm and laid a kiss there, then to her thumb, which he nipped with his teeth. Her eyes fluttered shut and he felt her pulse kick up another notch beneath his fingertips.

'It was more than that,' she said throatily.

Frustration sliced through him. 'Desire is a powerful drug. Especially for someone who has no experience.'

'I'd met men I liked before,' she contradicted, dropping her gaze to the bed. He didn't want her to hide herself from him. It frustrated him. 'It wasn't like I hadn't ever been tempted by a guy. Or fantasised about what it might be like…'

Jealousy again. It was as unwelcome now as it had been earlier.

'But with you it was so different. It was as though everything I am was bound up in being with you. I felt like I needed you in the same way I need breath and water.'

'That is what it should be like,' he murmured, for it had been exactly like this for him, with Frankie.

'Like what should be like?'

'When you go to bed with someone, it should be because you want them with an intensity that almost fells you at the knees.' He regarded her with all the need he felt in that moment—and it was more than strong enough to cut his body in two.

Her cheeks flushed pink. 'So you…feel that…have felt that before? Before me?' She cleared her throat. 'With other women?'

So much was riding on that question—her hopes were so raw they hurt him. And so he lied, because it was the kindest thing for her. He lied because if he told her that he'd never felt desire like he'd known that night, like he'd known with Frankie, she would see something more in that—she would see a promise he would never give. 'Yes.' His eyes dropped to her lips and he thought about kissing her, he thought about showing her that nothing mattered more than their desire for one another. But she'd made her feelings clear and he had to respect them, even when it was practically killing him. 'That's what good sex is about.'

It was a dream he'd had hundreds of times. He was back in the car, the smell of burning hair and flesh, of smoke and smouldering metal all around him. Adrenalin raced through his veins as the limousine filled with flames. He was trapped. He knew this feeling well. He pushed at his belt; it didn't move.

His eyes were scratchy—the smoke, he knew now.

His parents were dead, in the front of the car. His chest heaved as he looked towards them, saw his mother's beautiful face frozen still, horror on her features, almost as though she'd fallen asleep in the midst of a nightmare.

He turned to Spiro, bracing himself, wishing he could wake up, wishing he could reach back through time, into this dream, into the reality that had spawned it, and *do something*. But there was nothing—he was forced to relive this event again and again, the moment in which he had become truly alone.

Only Spiro wasn't there! Beside him, their faces bloodied, were Frankie and Leo.

He tasted vomit in his mouth and he stretched the belt, but it wouldn't move. His broken arm was an encumbrance he had no time for. With a curse, he called her name, but she didn't move. Leo was still, like a mannequin, so tiny, so frail.

He reached out and his fingertips curled around her fine blonde hair, clumped with blood, and blood filled his nostrils and eyes, vomit rushed through him. 'Frankie!' He called her name, urgently now, desperately, pushing at the seat belt again.

Nothing.

He was weak—powerless to help her.

Desperation tore him apart. 'Frankie!'

She lifted her head and looked at him, only her eyes were not green now, they were dark like Spiro's had been, like Leo's were. 'You can't save us,' she murmured, rejection in her features. 'Just let us go. Let me go.'

He woke then, his forehead beaded in perspiration,

his skin white. He turned towards Frankie on autopilot and almost cried out at the sight of her, fast asleep. But the dream was too real, the memory of it fractured and splintering into this time and life. 'Frankie.' He reached over and shook her arm.

She made a small noise then blinked her eyes open, looking at him.

'Matt?' In that tired, half-fogged state, she called him by the name he'd given her in New York. 'Is it Leo? What's wrong?'

Slowly, his breathing returned to normal. He looked at her for several seconds, reassuring himself that she was fine, and then he shook his head. 'Go back to sleep, Frankie. Everything's fine.'

Frankie stared at the little white bandage on her son's arm with a growing sense of rage and impotence. 'Liana—' she spoke slowly, in contrast to the way her temper was firing out of control '—what's this?'

Liana's eyes didn't quite meet Frankie's. 'From the doctor.'

'I see.' Frankie nodded, her chest heaving. She was getting married in the morning, and the last week had been both exhausting and distracting. She'd had less time for Leo than she would have liked, but she'd promised herself it would all go back to normal after the wedding. A new kind of normal, but normal nonetheless.

'Ouchie,' Leo said, looking up at his mother with big grey eyes and pointing to his arm. '*Big* ouchie.'

Frankie's heart cracked. 'Yes, I'll bet.' She bent down and kissed her son on the cheek. He returned to his drawing. Frankie straightened and looked at Liana. 'Excuse me.'

She spun away from the older woman, striding out of the room and moving until she reached a guard. 'Where is Matthias? Where is the King?'

The guard looked somewhat surprised; she suspected her temper was showing.

'Ah, he is…occupied,' the guard apologised.

She pulled herself up to her full, not very imposing height and stared down her nose at him. 'Where. Is. My. Fiancé?'

The guard flinched and spoke into the little device at his wrist. Crackly words came back and then he nodded. 'He is in the west garden. I'll show you.'

Frankie didn't smile. She was seething. How dared Matthias take Leo's blood without so much as telling her? How dared he take her son's blood *at all*? Damn him and his DNA test!

Her anger seethed the entire way, through the palace and out of enormous glass doors, into a garden that was overgrown with oak trees and flowers. It was very beautiful. At the bottom there was a tennis court and Matthias stood down one end, hitting balls that were being served to him by a machine. As she approached, her eyes swept the surroundings—she had become adept at seeking out security guards now.

'Have us left in privacy,' she said curtly, not much caring who heard her dress down the King, but knowing on some level that the words she wanted to spit at him would be more satisfying if she could give full vent to her rage and that spectators would hold her back. Slightly.

'Ah, yes, madam.' The guard bowed and spoke into his wrist once more. Two guards stepped out of the periphery of the tennis court, moving towards their location.

Here, in the inner sanctum of the palace, security was lessened. No one could reach these parts without high-level clearance.

Frankie waited until the guards had moved back to the palace and then she closed her eyes and saw her son's little arm, imagined a needle going into his flesh, sucking blood into vials for the purpose of confirming something that any idiot with eyes in their head could easily see. And rage flooded her once more. She stormed across the lawn and slammed open the wire gate to the tennis court.

A tennis ball flew from the machine and Matthias whacked it hard, landing it with speed in the opposing side's corner.

'I need a word with you,' she snapped, crossing to the machine and staring at it. 'How do I turn this damned thing off?' She looked towards him expectantly. His eyes were watchful, his expression bland. He reached into his pocket, pulled out a small device and pressed a button. The machine went quiet.

'Yes?' he asked, still so damned calm; she wanted to shake that nonchalance from his shoulders.

'You had my son's blood taken without even telling me?'

He walked across the tennis court, his stride lithe, wearing only a pair of white shorts and a white shirt

that clung to his broadly muscled chest. He was per-
spiring, the heat of the day intense, the tennis court in
the full baking sun.

'I did tell you,' he said as he placed the racket
down against the net and then came to stand in front
of Frankie. His eyes skimmed her face, then dropped
lower, before lifting to her eyes once more.

'When? When did you tell me you were going to
get some doctor to do something so—so—invasive?'

His frown was infinitesimal. 'It is not invasive. Just
a prick of a needle. The skin was numbed first and
Liana was with him the whole time. She said he felt
not a thing…'

'My God!' She stared at him as though he were some
kind of alien. 'You didn't even go with him?'

His laugh was a short bark. 'My schedule is rather
busy, *deliciae.*'

'That's your *son*!' she shouted, and rage pummelled
her insides so she lifted her palms and pushed at his
chest. His body was like steel, not moving, not so much
as an inch. She made a guttural sound and pushed
harder. Her rage grew.

'I am aware of that.' He spoke slowly. Calmly. 'I explained why the blood test was necessary.'

'But you didn't tell me *when* and I had no idea! I'm
his mom! That boy has never had a single procedure
in his life that I haven't been there for.' Hurt spun like
a web in her chest. 'Every headache, every nose bleed,
earache and injection, I have held his hand for. How
dare you keep this from me?'

'Calm down, Frankie,' he said quietly. 'This is not a big deal.'

'Not a big deal?' She glared at him and hands that had been pushing him formed fists and she pummeled his chest. He watched her, his expression impossible to interpret, and then, he caught her wrists and held them still. But her anger couldn't be stemmed. She stomped her feet and her fingers formed claws and she tried to break out of his grip but he held her completely still. She charged her body at his and he caught her then, wrapping his arms around her, holding her body tight to his.

'Let me go!' she screamed. 'I can't believe you did this. I can't believe you took his blood! I can't believe you think you had any right...'

'He is my son,' he said into her ear. 'And you understood why the paternity test was necessary...'

'He's not your son!' The words had the effect of surprising Matthias sufficiently that he loosened his grip on her. She jerked out of his grip and pushed at his chest once more for good measure. Her breathing was rushed, coming in fits and spurts. 'How can he be, when you can speak of him with such callous disregard? You organised for a doctor to do something to a little boy that would have been terrifying and you didn't even go along yourself? Or tell his mother? What a heartless, unfeeling lump you are!'

A muscle jerked in his jaw. He stared at her without moving.

'You don't feel a damned thing, do you?' she demanded again, glaring at him, and emotions, feelings, needs pushed through her, surging inside her. Whatever sentimentality he lacked, she more than made up for. 'God, what an idiot I am to think you could ever change.' She stared at him with a falling heart.

He grunted something, words she didn't catch, and then he moved to her, pulling her around her waist towards his body and holding her there. He stared down at her and, before she could guess his intention, he'd dropped his mouth to hers, kissing her, punishing her, tasting her, tormenting her.

She groaned, but it was an angry groan, and then she was kissing him back, harder, punishing him right back, wanting to hurt him with the intensity of her kiss. Her hands ripped at his shirt, pushing at him impatiently. Anger seemed to have been the straw breaking the camel's back and all the feelings she had worked so hard to hold off flooded through her.

She was furious! She was so furious! But desire was lurching inside her and she didn't want to ignore it. She wanted to use it to silence her rage!

'I hate you,' she said and in that moment she did. He stilled momentarily, then leaned down and lifted her, wrapping her legs around his waist. The power of his arousal did something to her body, weakening her, tempting her. 'I hate you,' she said again, but her mouth dropped to his shoulder, kissing his naked flesh even as her throat was raw with the ferocity of her anger.

'Good,' he said darkly, and she was so angry she didn't hear the resigned acceptance in his voice. 'So you should.'

She tasted his emotions; she felt them in every desperate lashing of his tongue, in the intensity of his grip around her waist, in the strength of his arousal. He felt—he just didn't know what to do with those feelings.

And she didn't care.

Thought had been put aside. Sense and reason were nowhere in evidence. All Frankie could do was feel and want.

She pushed at his chest and, with frustration, wriggled out of his arms; he guided her back to the ground, his eyes seeking hers for a moment. She ignored his look. She ignored everything. Her fingertips found his shorts and pushed at them; he stepped out of his shorts and shoes and then he pushed at her underpants, jerking them down her legs with impatience and desperation. She kicked them off but before her hands could find the zip of her skirt he'd lifted her once more, his eyes hunting hers with a question.

Her doubts had evaporated. She had only room for anger and need. She swore under her breath and nodded, biting down on her lower lip. 'Yes,' she groaned, as he moved her over his arousal and pushed inside her.

Her groan grew louder as pleasures so long denied moved through her body, and she remembered this. The intensity of his possession—the perfection of melding their two bodies into one.

He thrust into her, one hand on the back of her head, fingers pushing through her hair, dislodging it from the elegant style it had been put into that morning, the other hand clamped around her bottom, holding her where she was.

But it wasn't enough; she wanted so much more. With a grating cry she pushed at his chest and he stared at her for a moment, lost and confused. 'Lie down,' she commanded, and he did, pulling out of her for one devastating moment before they were one again, on the ground of the tennis court, the grass scratchy beneath her knees as she took him deep inside and rolled her hips, the power of this something she couldn't—wouldn't—ever forget. Beneath her, she saw his face grow pale and his breathing rushed, she saw desperate need fire in his veins and triumph was her companion.

Except there was no triumph in this—because she had lost. He had won. Sex was sex—there was no love in this.

She ignored the thought; the emotions it brought clawed at her throat and they were useless and unwelcome. She stared down at him, stilling slightly. 'Tell me this is meaningless,' she challenged, the gamble one she hadn't even known she was going to make. 'Tell me this means nothing.'

His eyes flared when they latched onto hers.

'Tell me while you're inside of me that this means nothing. That I mean nothing.' She felt tears slide down her cheeks, hot and fat. He caught her wrists and rolled her, flipping her onto her back and holding her still.

He moved inside her, gently at first, and then he kissed her slowly, trapping her beneath his body. Grief was equal to her desire. When would it not be?

He was skilled. Experienced. Despite the raging emotions in her chest, pleasure was inevitable. He rolled his hips and a wave began to build inside her, driving her to the edges of sanity, tipping her over it. She gripped his shoulders and he moved deeper. She cried his name out, over and over, as she fell apart.

But there was no recovery. No time to process what had happened. He kissed her lower, on her throat, and then his hands moved to the waistband of her shirt, pushing under it and finding the lace cups of her bra.

She was incandescent with pleasure. As he drove her to the edge, she kissed him harder and he kissed her right back. They tumbled off the edge of the world as they knew it, together. He exploded with the force of a thousand suns, their climax mutual and devastating.

And entirely inevitable, just as he'd always said.

CHAPTER ELEVEN

INSANITY HAD BROUGHT them together but it was dissipating quickly, leaving only confusion and regret in its wake. His body was heavy on hers and in another world, at another time, she would have lain beneath him all day, stroking his back, feeling him, wanting him anew.

But rage had been the catalyst for this and, with sensual heat evaporating, her rage surged afresh.

'I can't believe you did that.'

He pushed up on his elbows and looked at her with eyes that showed emotion—just not emotion she could make any sense of. 'You were…that was mutual.'

Her stomach plunged. 'I don't mean sex. I mean the blood test.'

Relief flashed on his features briefly and he lifted himself off her, extending a hand in an offer of assistance she ignored. She stood on her own and stared down at her outfit—it was in disarray. Shooting him a fulminating glare, she straightened her skirt and tucked her shirt back in place. Her underpants were across the tennis court; she wouldn't degrade herself by going in search of them.

He expelled a sigh. 'My parliament requires it. We've discussed that. It is done now, in any event. There is no sense arguing over an event neither of us can change.'

It was as simple as that to Matthias. Simple, pragmatic, black and white. Just like their marriage. Just like everything. 'You're unbelievable,' she muttered, looking towards the fairy tale palace with eyes that had started to see things as they really were. 'I thought this marriage made some kind of sense,' she whispered, letting her eyes close, and her heart close with them. 'I thought I could live with it. And maybe *I* can.' She could already see how addictive sleeping with Matthias would be. But it wasn't enough. Every time would destroy her a little more. 'But Leo shouldn't have to. Leo… Leo deserves so much better than this.'

There was silence. A heavy silence that throbbed with anger and disbelief. When she looked at him again he'd pulled his shorts on, but his chest was bare so she saw the way it heaved in an attempt to calm his breathing. Finally, he spoke. 'We are getting married *tomorrow.*'

'But we'll never be a family, will we?' The words were raw, thick with emotion.

The sun sliced across him, warm and bright. 'You will be my wife, and Leo is my son…'

'Sure he is,' she snapped. 'Once you have the DNA test results.'

Matthias's expression darkened. 'A DNA match will make him my legal heir; it will satisfy parliament. I do not need it to know who he is. Leo is my son. That fact has never been in dispute.' He spoke softly, perhaps attempting to soothe her, but it didn't work. She was beyond mollification.

'You'll never love me,' she said quietly. 'Will you?'

His expression flared with something like panic and her heart shattered. Yet she held her breath and she waited and she watched and, stupidly, she hoped. Finally, he shook his head. 'Love is not any part of this, as I have said all along.'

It hurt more than it should have. After what had just happened, she felt the rejection more keenly than anything else.

'And it never will be?' A glutton for punishment, apparently, she needed him to speak frankly. For him to be completely honest with her.

'No.'

So emphatic! So certain!

'So what just happened between us meant nothing to you?'

His square jaw tightened as he looked away from her. He was silent, and she took that silence as confirmation. It nearly tore her in half.

'And what about Leo?' she prompted, remembering his little bruised arm with fresh hurt. 'You do love him, don't you?'

The pause might as well have been an axe dropping. All her hopes crumbled in that moment. Reality was a pointed blade, one for which she had no shield.

'He's my son.' There was fear in Matthias's dark, swirling eyes. Fear and panic.

'For God's sake, he's not a damned possession!' she spat, forgetting her dislike for curse words and giving into the torrent of rage flowing through her like lava. 'He's not an accessory you can just put on a damned shelf! Leo is a living boy, a flesh and blood kid who doesn't give a care about your throne and your traditions and your damned cold heart! All he wants is to have a mum and a dad to play with—parents who adore him and are proud of him, who want to spend *time* with him, and delight in his achievements.'

A muscle jerked in his jaw and he spoke slowly, as though his own temper was pulling at him, begging to be indulged. 'That is not the way of royalty.'

'Says who?' she demanded. 'What was your own childhood like? I don't believe it was as cold as you are suggesting Leo's should be.'

'What do you know of my childhood?' he asked, deceptively calm.

She slammed her lips together and then her anger fired up anew. 'Nothing. But I know what mine was like. I know that my parents loved me even when they had no reason to.' Her eyes narrowed. 'I was given away, Matthias, by people who found it as easy to turn off their hearts as you apparently do, and I don't much like the idea of Leo *ever* knowing what that feels like.'

'Given away by whom?' he snapped, not understanding her implication.

'By my birth parents,' she returned, spinning away from him, her eyes caught by the hedge that grew around the tennis court.

'You're adopted?' he repeated, the words flattened of emotion.

'Yes.' There was defiance in her tone.

'Why have you never mentioned this before?'

'It didn't come up,' she said, and then bit down on her lower lip. 'And because I'm... I've lived with this shame, Matthias.' She whirled around to face him and pressed her fingertips between her breasts, as though she could score her way to her heart. 'I've lived with the knowledge that the people who should have loved me most in this world, and wanted me, didn't.'

A muscle jerked in his jaw and sympathy crossed his handsome face. 'I wish you'd told me this sooner.'

'Why?' she whispered. 'What difference does it make?'

They stared at each other in silence and then he moved closer, but she stiffened because her temper couldn't be restrained. Nor could her hurt.

'It is a part of you,' he said finally. 'A part of the woman you've become. It has been hurting you, and I would have liked... I would have liked to talk to you about it, to help you not suffer because of a decision two people made twenty-four years ago.'

'You make it sound like selling a house,' she muttered, shaking her head. 'My own parents didn't want me.' Her eyes were flinty when they lifted to his. 'Imagine what that feels like, then imagine how much I *don't* want Leo to ever know this pain.'

Her words lashed the air between them, and he stiffened visibly.

'People put their children up for adoption all the time,' he observed quietly. 'Oftentimes, because it is best for the child. Has it never occurred to you that your birth parents felt they were doing the right thing by you?'

'Of course it's occurred to me.' Her words were thick

with emotion. 'I've spent my whole life trying to understand why my own mother didn't want me.' To her chagrin, the sentence burned in her throat, emotion making the words dense and acidic. 'I was determined I wouldn't repeat whatever mistake my biological parents made.' Her eyes assumed a faraway look. 'I always thought that when I had a family, it would be with a man I could spend the rest of my life with. A man I respected. A man who loved me too much to ever let me go. I thought that when I started a family, it would be with someone who would love my children like they were his purpose for living. Nothing less would be acceptable for me or whatever children I might have. I thought I'd fall in love and get married and I'd finally feel like… I'd finally feel like…' She had to suck in a deep breath to stave off a sob. 'I thought I'd feel wanted.'

The words stung the air around them, whipping through the atmosphere.

'*Deliciae*—' But what could he say? He wanted her for her son. He'd made that obvious from the moment he'd approached her.

Tears sparkled on her long lashes. 'And then I met you and all my thoughts of saving myself for marriage went out the window. I discovered I was pregnant and had to face the reality of raising my child on my own.' She dashed at the tears that were threatening to run down her cheeks. 'It wasn't what I wanted, but I figured I could still give Leo the best of everything. And he had my parents, who loved me when they had no reason to.'

Matthias was as still as a statue, watching her with fierce concentration.

'Never would I have thought I'd be bringing my child up as a prince, the heir to a man who won't ever give him the love he deserves. A man who doesn't know how to love his own son.'

And now fresh tears ran down her cheeks, and Frankie didn't check them. She returned Matthias's gaze, her heart breaking, her soul splitting.

'I have never lied to you,' he said eventually, and she swept her eyes shut resignedly.

'I know that.' Her chest heaved. 'I knew it was unlikely you'd ever love me and, believe me, I have grappled with that fact. I have known that, in agreeing to this, I am consigning myself to the exact fate I've always sworn to avoid. You, and this marriage, are everything I didn't want for myself.' She straightened her spine, squaring her shoulders. 'But for Leo, to give him the father he deserves, I was prepared to put all that aside. What do my feelings matter when I can give him everything he should have?'

Matthias's eyes drew together, his expression not shifting. 'And what will he miss out on, living here with me? He is the Crown Prince of Tolmirós. He will want for nothing.'

'Come on, Matthias, don't be so obtuse. Children don't care about *things*. They don't care about *power*. He's just a sweet little kid, who wants to be loved. It's as easy as that.'

'I will do everything in my power to care for our son, you know that. I told you I will protect him with my dying breath…'

She shivered visibly. 'Do you think that's enough?'

His eyes glinted and slowly he nodded. 'It has to be. It is what I am offering.' He moved closer, so close they were almost touching and she could see the tiny flecks of silver in his dark eyes. 'I am what I am. I have never lied to you—I will never lie to you. I have been very careful never to make promises to you that I cannot keep.'

She bit down on her lower lip to stop it from trembling.

'I am telling you now that I will give our son a home, a future, and we will raise him as a family, just as I have always said.' His back was rigid, braced like steel. 'Our relationship is a separate concern to Leo's place here— as my son, and as my heir.'

'It's all the same thing,' she denied, shaking her head.

'No.' He lifted a hand, curling it around her cheek, stroking his thumb over her lips. 'You're offended I am not claiming to be in love with you,' he said quietly. 'And you're trying to hurt me by making that about Leo.'

'No!' she volleyed back urgently. 'I would never use our son in that way!'

He didn't relent. 'I have wondered why you are so hell-bent on idealism and commitment—why would a beautiful young woman deny herself the pleasure of sex in this day and age? And now I see. It is because you are always looking for a guarantee of security, for a promise you will not be abandoned again. You thought saving yourself for marriage would be an insurance policy of permanence.'

She drew in a harsh, raw breath at his accurate appraisal.

'You want to pick the safe option always, because

you were put up for adoption and you want to make sure nothing like that will ever happen to you again.'

She opened her mouth to deny it, but the words were locked in her throat.

'How can you not see that marriage without love is a safer bet than one predicated on emotion? Emotions fade and change. How can you not see that what I am offering you is everything you want?'

Her eyes sparkled and her beautiful face fell. She shook her head slowly from side to side, but bravely held his gaze. 'If you think any of this is what I want, then you know nothing about me.'

CHAPTER TWELVE

'Do you think this marriage is what *I* wanted?'

'I know it's not,' she conceded, and the pain in her pinched expression practically tore him in two.

'I wish, more than anything, that you could have everything you've just described. I wish you could have met a man who deserves you.' He knew, as he spoke the sentence, that it was the truth. That he wasn't—and never had been—worthy of Frankie. 'I wish you hadn't met me. I wish I'd done what I knew I should have and left you alone three years ago.' He ground his teeth together. 'Hell, Frankie, do you think I haven't woken up every day regretting what I require of you? Regretting the fact that I am forced to marry you even when I know it's the last thing you want?'

'Then why are you?' she whispered.

'You know the answer to that.' His jaw was firm. 'I cannot let Leo go. He must be raised here, by you, and as my son and heir. Neither you nor I has any say in this.'

A small sound escaped her, and he thought it might have been a sob.

'I can't live here with you.' She pulled away from him, taking a step backwards.

'You must,' he said darkly, wondering at the way his stomach seemed to be swooping and tightening constantly. 'Marriage is the only option open to us.'

She nodded jerkily and she stared at him with an attempt at strength and defiance that made him feel even worse. 'I'm aware of that. I have no interest in depriving our son of a birthright he would more than likely choose for himself when he comes of age.'

Matthias tilted his head in concession, hiding the look of darkness that moved over his features.

'When you suggested this marriage, you told me I could live at another palace.'

'Mare Visum.' He remembered the conversation, and the fact he had made the promise in good faith. He hadn't cared where she might choose to live at that point. And now?

Matthias did care. He thought of her living on another island, separated from him by sea and miles, and he wanted to reject the suggestion outright.

'Leo and I will go there after the wedding,' she said, her voice almost completely steady, her eyes unflinching.

'Running away?'

She let out a small sigh and when she spoke it was with an impatience that made him feel about as big as an ant. 'I'm trying to find a way to make this work. If I was going to run away, I would have done it by now, believe me.'

Respect lifted within him, even as he warred with

her words internally. To install Leo and Frankie in another palace did make perfect sense. They could spend their days happily, settling into a new lifestyle and culture, and he could continue as before. Nothing needed to change, except his country would rejoice in the knowledge of a blood heir to the throne.

It made sense. So why did he want to rail against the idea and refuse her suggestion? Why did he want to tell her he would never let his wife and child reside in a different palace to him?

The temptation to do just that terrified him, and so he nodded brusquely before he could give vent to the words that were racing through him. 'Fine.' He nodded. 'As you wish. After the wedding reception, you can be quietly moved to Mare Visum. Will this make you happy?'

For a moment her brave mask crumbled and she looked equal parts terrified and devastated. 'I'll make it work.' And then her expression hardened, like flint. 'You were right, Matthias. It turns out I'm capable of being a realist after all.' And she turned her back on him, walking slowly and calmly off the tennis court. He watched her go and told himself this would be for the best. He watched her go and told himself this odd feeling of uneasiness would disappear, just as every other feeling always had before.

Frankie was always beautiful, but dressed as a bride, her hair styled, a tiara on her head, surrounded by flowers and well-wishers, she was as stunning as he'd ever seen her.

No, that wasn't quite true. He closed his eyes for a moment and remembered the first moment he'd seen her, with no make-up, nothing special about her hair or clothes, but a smile that could power a space shuttle, and his gut pulled.

He remembered the way she'd looked when they'd made love that first time, when her face had glowed pink with rapture, her green eyes fevered with pleasure, and he had to bite back an audible groan.

He remembered the way she'd looked when he'd made love to her the day before, on the tennis court. So angry, so beautiful, so desperate with longing: the same longing that had carved him in two a long time ago.

But, while Frankie was beautiful now, there was a sadness in her features that cut through him.

He'd caused it. He'd caused it when he'd rejected her, just as she'd dreaded. He'd looked her in the eyes and told her he'd never really want *her*. He wanted their son, his heir, and she was a part of that deal.

All night it had swirled through his mind and he'd finally understood what had driven her outburst, what was at the root of all her reserve with him—she didn't want him to hurt her. She didn't want to care for him, to want him, to need him in any way, because she didn't trust him not to hurt her.

And because she wanted to be loved, and knew he'd never give her that.

Her green eyes were stormy, her lips tight, her skin pale. Standing as close as they were, at the front of the *cathedrali*, he could detect faint silver patches beneath her eyes, showing that she'd tossed and turned all night.

Though she was smiling, it was unnatural and forced and there was a faint tremor in her hands as she held them clasped in front of her.

Perhaps he was the only one in the cathedral who would detect these insignificant changes but, knowing what was in her heart, hearing how she felt, knowing that this marriage was the diametric opposite of everything she'd ever wanted and that she was going through with it regardless, something pulled in the region of his heart.

He looked around the beautiful ancient building—the place he'd come to bury his parents and brother, when he'd stood in this exact spot and spoken to reassure a panicked nation, and he channelled that same ability to quell his feelings, to silence his personal needs.

Today, as on that day, he was guided by what his people needed of him, but he was also led by what Frankie deserved, by how he could go some part of the way towards fixing this for her.

Frankie would become his Queen, and then he would let her go, allow her to live as private a life as she wished. In that one small way, he could give her what she needed.

'I, Frances Preston...' she spoke loudly, as clear as a bell, just as she'd been taught '...take you, Matthias Albert Andreas Vasilliás, to be my husband.' She was glad to be saying her vows because they were generally seen to be emotional and the fact that tears danced on her eyelashes would be regarded as natural and normal. 'I promise to be true to you in good times and in bad, in sickness and in health. I promise to love you and honour you, for as long as we both shall live.'

Relieved to have said her piece, she met his eyes and flinched almost instantly. A noise sounded: Leo. She looked towards him unconsciously and her skin goosebumped at the sight of their son, the boy who would be King one day, watching on with such joy. *Please let this be okay*, she prayed, sweeping her eyes shut.

'I, Matthias Vasilliás, take you, Frances Preston, to be my wife and Queen. I promise to be true to you at all times, when you are well, and when you are not.' Frankie held her breath, knowing what was to follow, bracing herself for how it would feel to have him say the words she desperately wanted to hear and know them to be false. 'I promise to love you and cherish you, for all the days of my life.'

She couldn't help it.

She lifted her eyes to his face and saw there that he was simply performing a part, and that he was as loath to say those words as she was to hear them. Her heart didn't break. It had broken already—how could it break further?

But it disintegrated within her, being swallowed into her bloodstream, leaving only cold acceptance in its wake.

This marriage was a fraud in every way. The fact their chemistry was off the charts was just as Matthias had always said. Sex was just sex.

And finally the last vestiges of her childish hopes and naïve dreams burst about her.

Somehow, seeing the reality, made it easier for her

to get through the rest of the ceremony. And, thankfully, the wedding reception was so full of dignitaries that there was always someone to talk to. Someone to dance with. Frankie took every opportunity she could to put some distance between herself and Matthias, doing whatever she could simply to pass the time, all the while knowing that she would soon be able to leave this damned palace, and her new husband, far behind.

She avoided him as best she could and she kept her heart closed off, but finally, at the end of the night, came the moment to dance with her husband. Every single guest and many of the palace servants stood at the edges of the enormous ballroom, and Frankie could fight it no longer.

For the next few minutes she had to pretend to be happy, and then they would leave and this would all be behind her.

Matthias walked to her with slow intent, his eyes holding hers in a way that made her blood gush and her chest hurt. He held a hand out and she placed hers in it, her stomach doing loops. She ignored those feelings and breathed out in an attempt to steady herself.

He led her to the middle of the dance floor and then the priest approached, a smile on his face showing they'd fooled him, at least. He held in his hands a small spool of silver thread. Once he was close enough he spoke soft words in Tolmirón, then began to loop the thread from her hand to Matthias's and back again. She remembered being told about this, but it had been so long ago she forgot the significance of it.

Some kind of tradition, though.

When their hands were bound tightly, the priest nodded and stepped away. Music began to play, soft and beautiful, and Matthias brought her closer to his chest, holding her there so she could hear the beating of his untouchable heart.

'This thread is from the Mediterranean silk crab,' he said. 'It is native to the caves of Tolmirós. Their silk grows deep beneath the ocean's surface. For as long as there are records, royal marriages have been blessed by this binding. It is said that dancing with the threads like this promises a long and happy marriage.'

Her fingers were aching beneath the beautiful silk. She inherently rejected everything he said.

'I see.'

She felt rather than heard his sigh. He didn't speak for the rest of the dance, but afterwards they stood with their hands bound, smiling at their guests.

'Is it over?' she asked quietly, her heart stammering inside her.

He tilted a glance at her, his face hiding whatever he was feeling, and then he nodded. 'We may leave.'

She kept her expression bland, her back straight, as they slipped out of the crowded ballroom to cheers and applause from all assembled. She walked beside him through the ancient corridors of the palace but as soon as they rounded the corner and were in the privacy of their residence at last, she pulled at her hand.

It wouldn't come loose. She pulled again, lifting her other hand to rip the threads free. Only they wouldn't disentangle, and it was suddenly almost impossible for Frankie to breathe.

'Please get this off,' she said, looking up at him with panic, pulling on it.

His alarm was obvious. 'Calm down, *deliciae*—'

'Don't call me that. Please. Get it off. I can't... I can't... I can't breathe.' She bit down on her lip, pulling on her hand until he held her still.

'You're only making it tighter. Just be still.'

But she couldn't. She kept pulling and he swore, reaching out and curling his fingers around her chin. 'You must be still.' He spoke loudly and firmly so that she stopped struggling and stood, her teeth chattering and her stomach in knots. Watching her the whole time, he eased a finger beneath the threads and found the loose end. He unthreaded them as quickly as he was able, but it still took longer than a minute and in that time Frankie's panic only rose, her huge eyes darkening, her face draining of colour. Finally, when he was almost done, she pulled at her hand and rubbed it in front of her.

'It's just threads,' he said in an apparent attempt to reassure her.

Only it wasn't just threads. They were married now, bound in all the ways a man and a woman could be united: tied together for life by law and by a child and, for Frankie, by love. But her love wasn't enough. It never had been—it never would be.

She needed to get away from him as soon as possible.

He glared at the painting and, for the hundredth time in the four weeks since Leo and Frankie had left the palace, contemplated moving it. He knew he should.

He knew it had no place in his life, let alone here in the place he undertook important government work.

The painting had always been a distraction, from the day it had arrived, but at least before it had been a pleasant distraction. Now it served only to plunge him into a black hole of anger, a deep place of desolate realism.

She was gone.

It had been four weeks.

He turned his attention to the documents in front of him and read them again, then, with an impatient thrust of his hand, pushed them away. It was barely afternoon, but he stood and crossed to the bar on the other side of the room and poured himself a stiff measure of whisky. He inhaled it, then threw it back, his hand slightly unsteady when he refilled the glass.

What time had he gone to bed the night before? Three? Four?

He couldn't recall.

He glared at the painting from up close, seeing the brushstrokes and imagining the way her hand would have moved as she painted it. He hated the painting in that moment with a visceral rage because it embodied so much of who Frankie was, what she was, and he'd never felt more distant from her—nor that she was more out of his reach.

A knock sounded on his door. He ignored it; the knock came again.

'What?'

His valet Niko entered, holding a brown envelope. 'Today's security memo.' Niko placed the envelope on the desk and turned to leave.

Matthias grunted by way of acknowledgement, turning his gaze to the large envelope.

They'd been gone four weeks and in that time he hadn't called her once. He'd resisted every single urge to pick up the phone and speak to her. Any time he'd thought of so much as dialling Mare Visum palace to see how she was, to speak to Leo, he'd recalled the sight of Frankie trying to pull her hand free from their ceremonial wedding bind; he'd sensed her panic and despair and he'd known that to call her would be selfish. To speak to her might improve his spirits, might reassure him that she was making sense of their new lives, but it would hurt her, he was sure of that.

And so he'd ordered security packets. Daily. It was a way to stay informed of her movements. To see her life unfurl.

He crossed to the desk now, his stride long, his fingers moving deftly as they tore the top off the envelope.

Usually the envelope included a single A4 piece of paper with a typewritten, lacklustre report of Frankie and Leo's movements. But when he reached into the envelope for the memo, he pulled out a newspaper article as well. With a frown, his eyes ran over the words, a sense of disbelief scrambling through him.

Eggs for the Prince! the headline screamed.

Matthias read the short article, describing the delight of a local café operator who'd discovered that the beautiful blonde woman and adorable dark-haired boy who'd wandered in for breakfast the day before were, in fact, Her Majesty the Queen and the young Crown Prince.

The photos, snapped on cell phones by nearby diners, obviously, showed Frankie and Leo doing nothing more exciting than eating breakfast. Nor did it show a single security guard anywhere nearby. She wore a baseball cap low on her brow, her ponytail pulled through the back, and Leo was wearing sunglasses.

So far as disguises went, it was pretty simple.

Matthias could tell it was his wife and son.

His *wife*.

He glared at the picture and his chest ached as though it were being scraped out and emptied completely of contents.

She'd wanted to be left alone, but he'd believed she would act in their child's best interests. To take him out without any protection detail… What the hell was she playing at?

Anything could have happened! Kidnap! Murder! An accident! And she'd accused him of not caring about Leo?

He ground his teeth together and, before he could realise what he was doing, he pulled Frankie's painting off the wall and hurled it across the room, satisfied when the frame cracked upon landing. He stared at it, broken and damaged, something that had once been so beautiful and pleasing, and tried not to draw a comparison to Frankie. He told himself he was glad. The painting was nothing but a damned distraction and he was done being distracted by this.

But the longer he stared at it, the more his gut twisted, until he felt only shame.

Shame, and a deep, profound sense of grief.

He swore in his native tongue and scooped down, picking the pieces up, trying to shape it back together, almost as though a madness of sorts had descended upon him. 'Damn it,' he cursed again, when it wouldn't comply. He'd broken something beautiful. He'd broken it beyond repair.

Carefully, slowly, he placed the painting down on the desk, his powerful hands reverent with the frame where only a minute ago he'd lashed out, acting in anger.

Without thought, purely on instinct, he reached out, pressing a button on his phone; Niko answered almost immediately.

'Have the helicopter readied.'

'Yes, sir. What is your destination?'

He pressed a finger to the painting, feeling the ridges made by the layers she'd added, each with care, each with love, and his eyes closed of their own accord. He tilted his dark head back, his expression held tight.

'Mare Visum.'

The colours weren't right. She ran her brush over the top of the canvas, streaking a fine line of grey over the black, so fine it was almost translucent, giving it a pearlescent sheen. Better. But still not quite right.

She took a step back to study the painting, her frown deepening. There was a kind of magic about the moonlit nights here, on the southern tip of Tolmirós. She'd watched the moon coming over the ocean each night since coming to live in Mare Visum, and she'd tried to capture the ethereal quality on her canvas but, again and again, she'd failed.

With a grunt, she grabbed her cloth and swiped it over the bottom of the canvas, smearing the ocean she'd painted only the day before so it looked like a murky swamp, then dropping her head into her hands.

She was tired, that was all. She wasn't sleeping well.

Her stomach rolled as her mind immediately supplied the answer as to why that was.

Matthias.

Her fingers dug into her hair, pulling it loose from the braid, and she made a guttural, groaning sound of impatience. For God's sake, as if it wasn't bad enough that her dreams were tormented by memories of her husband; now he was invading her waking world?

She'd tried so hard to banish him from her thoughts.

But every time she thought she'd done it—gone an hour or two without her mind wandering to damned Matthias—he was there, his handsome face in full Technicolor in her mind's eye.

With another sound of impatience, she pulled her hands away from her face and stared at the painting, then grabbed her paintbrush, dipped it in the red oil paint and lifted it, striking a single angry line through the painting's middle.

Maybe her gift was now destroying art, rather than creating it?

She lifted her hand to mark the canvas again.

'Stop.'

His voice held her still instantly and she spun around, her eyes finding his in the doorframe. He was watching her with a stillness that made her heart do the exact opposite—it was pounding hard and fast inside her, so fast it made her knees shake. She hadn't seen him since their wedding; she had no time to prepare for seeing him now.

'Stop,' he said again, and she realised she was still holding the paintbrush in her fingertips like a sword, with blood at its tip. She dropped her gaze to it, her heart pounding, her mind racing. She sucked in a breath and looked at him once more, her expression giving little away.

'I wasn't aware you were coming to the palace,' she said, the words slightly stilted. 'I presume you've come to see Leo. He's asleep. But he'll be…'

Matthias began to walk into the room and she held her breath then, watching him as he came right in front of her and slowly took the brush from her hand.

'Stop,' he said quietly, for the third time, his eyes roaming her face, his features symmetrical, both familiar and unfamiliar to her. He stood so close she could feel warmth emanating from his powerful, broad frame, so close she could lean forward and touch him, so close she could inhale his intoxicating scent.

So close.

She shook her head slightly, taking a step backwards, and his hand shot out, steadying her before she could connect with the still-wet canvas.

His touch on her skin was like a thousand volts of electricity; it ripped through her and she clamped her mouth together to stop from letting out a groan.

Because she'd dreamed of his touch; she'd craved it to the point of insanity and despair. 'Don't,' she whispered, pulling away from him, turning her back on him and staring at the wasteland of the painting.

He was no longer touching her, but her arm felt warm where his fingers had connected with her. She swallowed in an attempt to bring moisture back to her mouth.

'Leo will be awake soon, if you want to wait in the lounge.' The words were brittle, like a porous old seashell left out in the sun.

'I came to see you.'

Her eyes swept shut at the declaration and she braced for whatever was going to come next. She had wondered how long she would be allowed to hide out like this, before being asked to return to some kind of normality, to the royal duties that accompanied her role. Only she'd expected it would be a lowly servant who would summon her back to the palace, back to her King's side.

She hadn't expected it to be Matthias.

She wasn't prepared for this.

'Why?' A hollow whisper.

He didn't speak. He said nothing and for so long that eventually she turned to face him, and now a spark of anger was igniting inside her. 'Why?' Louder. More demanding.

Because he'd invaded her sanctuary, and without any warning; he hadn't given her any chance to raise her defences and it wasn't fair.

She held onto that anger, using it, knowing how well it served her in that moment.

He opened his mouth to say something and then appeared to change his mind.

He moved closer, but not to her, towards the painting, and he frowned as he looked at it. Self-conscious—she never liked it when people looked upon her art as it was forming on the canvas—she felt almost as if she'd been walked in on while naked. A work in progress was raw, messy, chaotic.

She tried to see it through his eyes.

It was moody and atmospheric. The destruction she'd foisted on its lower half minutes earlier only added to its brooding intensity. The red line was striking.

'I bought it, you know,' he said, and she frowned because she had no idea what he was talking about. 'The painting you were working on when we met.'

'You… It sold to a private buyer.' She shook her head, lifting her eyes from the new painting to his taut profile.

'To me.' He looked towards her abruptly, so she had no chance to flick her gaze away. 'It sold to me.'

'Why? Why did you buy it?'

His smile was dark, self-deprecating, imbued with anger and scepticism. 'Because, Frankie, I found it very hard to put you out of my mind.' He spoke darkly. 'I bought it to challenge myself—you were always there with me, and yet I knew I could never contact you. I was testing my strength and resolve by keeping that beautiful piece you'd created close to me. Taunting myself with what I couldn't ever have again.'

It made absolutely no sense.

'You got into my bloodstream, like some kind of fever, and I refused to let you weaken me.'

She bit down on her lower lip, hurt shifting inside her. 'I didn't want to weaken you.'

'I know that.' He took in a deep breath, his chest moving with the action. 'I know that.' He lifted a hand then, as if to touch her cheek, but then took a step backwards, keeping his body stiff, his expression impossible to read. He was stern. Focused. She would have said *unemotional*, except she could feel waves of emotion emanating from him.

'You were at a café with Leo.'

There was a thick undercurrent to the words. They came to her from far away, making no sense. 'This morning?'

He gave nothing away. 'It was in the papers. A photograph of the two of you.'

'Yes.' She nodded, darting her tongue out and licking her lower lip. 'I was annoyed about that. I didn't notice a photographer.'

'Anyone with a cell phone is paparazzi these days.'

That was true. She nodded.

'Did you go out without security?'

The question caught her off-guard. 'I… It was… The island is tiny and the café an easy walk. Leo and I go to the beach often, without guards. I didn't think…'

And now, as though he couldn't help himself, he put his hands on her forearms and held her still. He stared down at her and she stared back, but her heart wouldn't stop racing; blood gushed through her so fast she could hear it roaring inside her ears like an angry ocean.

'You didn't think?' he asked, haunted, and he dragged her body to his, holding her against him, and she didn't fight him; she didn't even think about fighting him.

'What if someone wanted to hurt you? Or hurt him? What if someone kidnapped Leo?'

'I was with him the whole time,' she said shakily. 'Nothing was going to happen.'

'You don't know that,' he groaned, as though he could barely speak. 'You cannot take those kinds of risks, Frankie. You can't do it. Please. Please do not take these risks.'

'It's not a risk,' she promised softly, gently, her heart turning over for him.

'How do you know this?' His jaw tightened as though he were grinding his teeth. 'You can't. You're acting on blind faith and I am not prepared to. I won't live with this kind of worry. I can't.'

Sympathy curled inside Frankie. She reached up and ran her fingers over his cheek so his breath escaped him in a single hiss. 'I understand why you feel that way,' she said softly. 'You lost your family in terrible circumstances. You couldn't save them, and now you're worried something will happen to Leo and you won't be able to save him.' His eyes flared. 'But you can't keep him in some kind of gilded cage. Not here, not in your home. I want him to have as normal a life as is possible. You have to trust that I can keep him safe. You have to trust me.'

She could see as each word hit its mark, she could see the way his face stretched with each statement. 'I have lost everyone I ever cared for,' he said finally, the words tight as though being dragged from him against his will. 'I have no intention of losing you or Leo.'

Stupid, blind hope beat inside her, but she refused to answer it.

'Tell me why,' she said, her whole body attuned to every movement of his.

'Tell you what?' He was guarded again, cautious. 'What do you want from me?'

She blinked thoughtfully. 'Tell me why you're so furious about this.'

'You are my wife—he is my son…'

She shook her head. It wasn't good enough. 'You were prepared to marry someone else two months ago,' she reminded him with steady determination. 'If something happened to us, you could simply remarry. Have another child.'

'Don't,' he ground out, and hope in her chest flared larger, brighter.

'What? You're a realist, remember? You can marry whomever you want and have as many children as you need. Why do you care about me and Leo?'

'He is my son!' The words were torn from him, and then he was dragging a hand through his hair, pulling at it, his eyes tortured, haunted, and she hated having to push him, but deep down she knew how essential it was.

'Yes, and you can't bear the thought of something happening to him, can you? It would kill you if he was hurt in any way?'

'Of course!' he roared. 'Damn it, Frankie, I'm done losing people I—'

'Say it,' she demanded, crossing her arms over her chest.

'I'm done losing people,' he finished, stepping back

from her, putting physical space between them as though that would defuse this.

Frankie wasn't going to back down though. 'I never expected you to take a coward's response, Matthias.'

'How dare you call me a coward?' He laughed, but it was a sound of desperation—a dying man trying to grab a life raft.

'I dare because I faced every single one of my fears when I married you. I married a man I love with all my heart, who claimed he'd never love me. I married you knowing I was relegating myself to a life of loneliness. I married you with only the smallest seed of hope that you might ever care for me how I needed you to. And now you won't even admit that you love our son? When it's the most natural thing in the world?'

He glared at her and her heart raced. 'I love him, okay? I love him so much I am terrified of how I'll live if anything ever happens to our child. I look at him and I see my brother—my brother as he was in the accident when I couldn't even reach him, I couldn't save him. I couldn't save them, Frankie. My whole family died and I couldn't do a damned thing. What if something happens to Leo?' He waved a hand over his eyes, then blinked at her with despair. 'What if something happens to you?'

She hated seeing him like this. She moved to him and put a hand on his shoulder but he stayed firm, unreceptive.

'Don't. I cannot ask you to reassure me, and I don't want to lie to you. I made a choice that first night I met you that I wouldn't love you, Frankie. I have made that choice all along, even when, yes—okay, fine—when every single cell in my body aches to say what you need to hear. Even when I know I probably fell in love with you the second we met.'

Frankie drew in a shaking breath.

'But I *chose* not to act on that. I chose not to let that control my actions.'

He stood before her, a king of men, and she saw only the fifteen-year-old he'd been.

She shook her head, lifting up on tiptoe and brushing her lips to his. He stood rock-still.

'I can't do this,' he said, but his hands lifted into her hair and held her where she was. He pressed his forehead to hers and she made a small sound, deep in her throat.

'You can't keep yourself shut off from life because of an accident,' she said simply when his pain was complex and ran so deep. 'Just like I can't live in fear of rejection all my life because my birth parents chose not to raise me. We neither of us need to be defined by our past, Matt.'

'When my family died—' he spoke quietly but their faces were so close she heard his words as though they were being breathed into her soul '—I wanted to turn my back on the kingdom. I wished I'd died too, Frankie. I wanted to die.'

'But you didn't. You became the leader they needed you to be...'

'Once. I did that once.' He pressed a kiss to her cheek and she turned her head, capturing his lips with hers. 'If anything ever happened to you and Leo, if I lost either of you, I don't think I could do this again.'

Her heart, so broken, so splintered, began to pull together and she knew then that she had to be strong—not just for herself, but for Leo and Matt as well. 'I can't promise nothing will ever happen to me. Or Leo. Life comes with so few guarantees. But Matt, you can't keep pushing us away. Not when we're right here, your wife and your son, so in love with you. You can't keep pushing us away just because something *might* happen, one day. You can't throw our family away because you're afraid. Not when, by being brave, there's a good chance we'll all get everything we ever wanted in life…'

He shook his head against hers, his hand moving to curl around her cheek, his other fastening around her back.

'I ruined it,' he said, the words husky.

She looked up at him, frowning.

'The painting. I was so… I do not know. Angry. Afraid. No, I was terrified. When I saw that newspaper article, I took the painting from the wall and threw it to the ground, and I stared at the broken frame, the once beautiful object I had destroyed because I was afraid, and I felt… I ruined the painting,' he said gruffly. 'And I cannot bear that I have ruined our marriage too. I cannot bear the idea that fear has made me hurt you and push you away, that I have put you through the kind of pain I have felt this last month…'

'You say fear, but I look at you and I see a man who is so brave. What you've been through and turned your life into? I don't know anyone else who could have done that.'

'Don't. Do not speak so highly of me when I have been a coward, pushing you away rather than admitting how I feel for you...'

'You came here today,' she said softly. 'You're here because you love me, aren't you?'

His eyes glistened black in his handsome face. 'Yes,' he said on a whoosh of relief, a smile crossing his face. 'I am.'

'Then you are brave,' she promised. 'And I love you.'

'How is it possible?' he asked, wonderment and weight in the question.

'Because you are good and kind and because I believe in fairy tales and for ever.' She pressed a kiss against his nose and his eyes fell closed. 'Because I'm an optimist, and because my heart is as much yours as it ever was.'

'Your heart is a fool,' he groaned huskily. 'To love a man so unworthy of you.'

'You are more worthy of me than you give yourself credit for.'

'I doubt that,' he said with a shake of his head. 'But I will spend the rest of my life trying to deserve you.'

He scooped down and lifted her up, cradling her against his chest, and she laughed at the sudden movement. 'What are you doing?'

'I have missed you, Frankie, in every single way. This last month has been an agony. I have longed to talk to you. To show you my kingdom—*our* kingdom. I have wanted to see your wonder as you discover what is so

special about Tolmirós, and I have missed Leo with an
intensity that is impossible to describe. I have missed
you in every way, and right now I want to make love to
you as I should have all along—hold you close and tell
you that I love you, tell you that everything you have
wanted all your life is right here. I want this day to be
the first day of your fairy tale, Frankie.'

'I thought you didn't believe in fairy tales,' she
couldn't help teasing.

'I didn't.' He was serious. 'Until I met you—and I
found myself living in one regardless.'

He kissed her then, a kiss of longing and love, and it
inflated her soul. 'You have given me everything I ever
wanted—my wife, my son, a family, a future. And I almost lost you because I couldn't admit that. I've been
such a *vlakás*.'

She had no idea what the word meant. 'Yes.' Her
agreement was sanguine as she wrapped her arms
around his neck. 'But I forgive you.'

'You were right about my upbringing,' he said
throatily. 'I don't often think about my childhood. I
try not to, anyway.' He furrowed his brow. 'But that
day, when you were so angry with me, you said my
childhood wasn't cold. That it was full of love. And
you were right. My mother adored Spiro and me. She
would have fought like a wildcat, as you did, to protect her children.'

Frankie's stomach churned with sadness for this
woman, this poor woman. 'I'd like to know more about
her,' she said honestly, and lifted her hand to his chest.
'I'd like to hear about your family.'

She could feel his resistance; she could see that it was something he was fighting, but then he nodded tightly. 'I think I'd like to talk to you about them. In time.'

It was enough. She lifted up and pressed a kiss to his cheek. 'We have all the time in the world, Matthias. I'm not going anywhere.'

EPILOGUE

NINE MONTHS LATER to the day, baby Emilia Vasilliás was born—a beautiful little sister for Tolmirós's thriving Crown Prince Leo.

Matthias had been by his wife's side the entire time—from the moment they'd discovered she was pregnant, only a week after her return to the palace, all the way to the delivery.

As he'd promised, in his office he was King, but he was also a man. A husband and a father, and as he watched her deliver him of another beautiful child he was mainly a bundle of nerves.

He hated seeing her in pain; he longed to be able to carry that pain, to experience it for her, so that she didn't need to feel the agony she was enduring. But she was so strong, so brave, and after hours of labour a baby's cry broke through the hospital and they looked upon their princess for the first time.

'She is beautiful, like you,' he said, the words thick as he placed the bundled-up child on his wife's chest.

Exhausted but delirious, Frankie stared at her daughter, emotions welling inside her. 'She's so like Leo was,'

Frankie murmured, a smile on her lips, tears on her lashes. 'The same little nose and look, your dimple,' she said, looking up at Matthias. Her heart exploded at the sight of the big, strong King with suspiciously moist eyes of his own.

'She is divine,' he agreed, the words thick with feeling. 'A princess for our people.'

'A sister for Leo.' Frankie grinned, stroking their baby's dark pelt of hair. She pressed a kiss to Emilia's forehead and then relaxed back against the bed. 'How perfect she is.'

'How perfect you are,' Matthias corrected, kissing Frankie's cheek. 'A true warrior queen.'

Their marriage was blessed with three more children— a family of seven—and each birth was rejoiced at and celebrated by the people of Tolmirós, just as the country cheered when Leo, a young man of twenty-eight, announced his engagement to an Australian doctor. His parents were beside him when he married, and by the time Leo welcomed his first child onto this earth, Matthias's life was so rich and full, his family so extensive, that he loathed to think of a time when he had almost turned his back on what could have been. He remembered, of course, the instinct to push Frankie away, to close himself off to love because he had lost so much once before.

But brave warrior Queen Frankie had seen through that and she'd fought for what they were, regardless of her own fears and insecurities. And for that he loved her almost more than anything.

Fairy tales generally ended with the idea of people living happily ever after, but Matthias no longer thought about endings—he thought about each day as it came, and he lived with gratitude and peace. Come what may, he had been blessed, and blessed again—more than all the fairy tales in all the land.

* * * * *

COMING NEXT MONTH FROM

H HARLEQUIN *Presents*®

Available June 18, 2019

#3729 THE GREEK'S PREGNANT CINDERELLA
Cinderella Seductions
by Michelle Smart

Tabitha is stunned to be gifted a ticket to Giannis's ball. But this untouched Cinderella ends up in his bed—utterly pleasured! She expects to return to her ordinary life...until Tabitha discovers a nine-month consequence!

#3730 HIS TWO ROYAL SECRETS
One Night With Consequences
by Caitlin Crews

For one passionate night in a stranger's arms Pia feels free...and then she learns she's carrying the Crown Prince of Atilia's twins! But Pia's true royal secret is that she's falling inescapably in love with her dark-hearted prince...

#3731 BOUGHT BRIDE FOR THE ARGENTINIAN
Conveniently Wed!
by Sharon Kendrick

Hired by Alejandro, executive Emily must redeem this playboy's reputation. She suggests he take a convenient wife to show he's changed. What she doesn't expect is Alejandro's insistence that *she* take on the role!

#3732 DEMANDING HIS HIDDEN HEIR
Secret Heirs of Billionaires
by Jackie Ashenden

Billionaire Enzo has never known a passion like the one he shared with Matilda. But she left abruptly... Now Matilda has reappeared— with his son! Enzo demands his heir, but will he claim vibrant Matilda, too?

HPCNM0619RA

#3733 HIS SHOCK MARRIAGE IN GREECE
Passion in Paradise
by Jane Porter

When tycoon Damen's convenient bride is switched at the altar for Kassiani, he's adamant their marriage will remain strictly business. He's too damaged for anything more... Yet will the intense passion of their honeymoon be his undoing?

#3734 AN INNOCENT TO TAME THE ITALIAN
The Scandalous Brunetti Brothers
by Tara Pammi

To uncover a business scandal, billionaire Massimo requires shy Natalie to play his fake fiancée. But this untamable Italian might have met his match in innocent Nat, who challenges him...and tempts him beyond reason!

#3735 WED FOR THE SPANIARD'S REDEMPTION
by Chantelle Shaw

The only way Rafael can become CEO is if he marries. He isn't the commitment kind, but he'll save single mother Juliet financially if she becomes his wife. But can Rafael keep their marriage purely for appearances?

#3736 RECLAIMED BY THE POWERFUL SHEIKH
The Winners' Circle
by Pippa Roscoe

Ten years ago, Mason was swept into an affair with Prince Danyl. Now he's back with a million-dollar demand she cannot refuse. Will their painful past be overcome by their intense desire?

YOU CAN FIND MORE INFORMATION ON UPCOMING HARLEQUIN® TITLES, FREE EXCERPTS AND MORE AT WWW.HARLEQUIN.COM.

HPCNM0619RB

Get 4 FREE REWARDS!

We'll send you 2 FREE Books plus 2 FREE Mystery Gifts.

Harlequin Presents® books feature a sensational and sophisticated world of international romance where sinfully tempting heroes ignite passion.

FREE Value Over $20

Billionaire Enzo has never known passion like what
he shared with Matilda. But she left abruptly…
Now Matilda has reappeared—with his son!
Enzo demands his heir, but will he claim vibrant
Matilda, too?

Read on for a sneak preview of
Jackie Ashenden's debut story for Harlequin Presents,
Demanding His Hidden Heir.

"*Bueno notte*, Mrs. St George," Enzo said in that deep voice she knew so
well, the one that had once been full of heat and yet now was so cold. "I
think you and I need to have a little chat."

"A chat?" she said huskily, her chin firming, the shock and fear in her
gaze quickly masked. "A chat about what?"

With an effort, Enzo dragged his gaze from her throat.

So, she was going to pretend she didn't know what he was talking
about, was she? Well, unfortunately for her, he wasn't having it.

"I'm not here to play games with you, Summer," he said coldly. "Or
should I say Matilda. I'm here to talk about my son."

Another burst of quicksilver emotion flashed in her eyes, but then it was
gone, nothing but a cool wall of gray in its place. "Yes, that's my name. You
don't have to say it like a pantomime villain. And as for a son… Well." Her
chin came up. "I don't know what you're talking about."

"Is that how you're going to play this?" He didn't bother to temper the
acid in his tone. "You're going to pretend you don't know anything about
that child you just rescued downstairs? The child with eyes the same color
as mine?" He took a step toward her. "Perhaps you're going to pretend that
you don't know who I am either."

She held her ground, even though she didn't have anywhere to go, not
when there was a wall behind her. "No, of course not." Her gaze didn't
flicker. "I know who you are, Enzo Cardinali."

The sound of his name in her soft, husky voice made a bolt of lightning
shoot straight down his spine, helplessly reminding him of other times
when she'd said it.

"Good." He kept his voice hard, trying not to let the heat creep into it. "Then if you know who I am you can explain to me why you didn't tell me that I have a son."

She was already pale; now she went the color of ash. But that defiant slant to her chin remained, the expression in her eyes guarded. "Like I said, I don't know what you're talking about."

Enzo's rage, already inflamed by his body's betrayal, curdled into something very close to incandescence, and it burned like fire in his blood, thick and hot.

He'd never been so angry in all his life, some distant part of him vaguely appalled at the intensity of his emotions—a reminder that he needed to lock it down, since his iron control was the only thing that set him apart from his power-hungry father.

But in this moment he didn't care.

This woman, this beautiful, sexy, infuriating woman, hadn't told him he had a son and, more, she'd kept it from him for four years.

Four. Years.

He took another step toward her, unable to help himself, the fire in his veins so hot it felt as if it was going to ignite him where he stood. "I see. So you are going to pretend you know nothing. How depressingly predictable of you."

"Simon is my son." Her hands had gone into fists at her sides and she didn't move, not an inch. "And H-Henry's." Her gaze was as cool as winter rain, but that slight stutter gave her away.

"No." Enzo kept his voice honed as a steel blade. "He is not. Those eyes are singular to the Cardinali line. Which makes him mine."

"But I—"

"How long have you known, Matilda? A year? Two?" He took another step, forcing her back against the wall.

Enzo put a hand on the wall at one side of her silky red head and leaned in close so she had no choice but to stare straight at him. "Look at me, *cara*. Look at me and tell me that you don't see your son staring back."

Don't miss
Demanding His Hidden Heir,
available July 2019 wherever
Harlequin® Presents books and ebooks are sold.

www.Harlequin.com

HARLEQUIN

Presents®

**Coming next month—
a passionate marriage-of-convenience romance!**

In *Bought Bride for the Argentinian* by Sharon Kendrick, Emily is reunited with Alejandro, the enigmatic playboy from her past. But what she doesn't expect is for their reunion to end in marriage…!

Alejandro Sabato, the unforgettable man from her past, has hired PR executive Emily Green to redeem his playboy reputation. She suggests he take a convenient wife to show he's changed. What she doesn't expect is Alejandro's insistence that *she* take on the role! Emily's dangerously aware of the enduring desire still sparking between them. But can she risk her heart again when she's only a bride on paper…?

Bought Bride for the Argentinian

Conveniently Wed!

Available July 2019

HPBPA0619